"Can You J[...] From This?"

"It's just physical reaction," Hillary insisted.

Troy stepped in front of her. "Hillary, damn it... You confuse the hell out of me. I'm worried about you, and hell yes, I want to make love to you. But I also want time with you."

"Honestly?"

"Spend a week with me. Get me out of your system so you can return to your regular life without regrets."

"What makes you think you're in my system?"

"Really? Are you going to look me in the eye and tell me you don't feel the attraction, too? Remember, I was there when we kissed."

"Okay, I'll admit there's...chemistry."

"Explosive chemistry..."

Dear Reader,

Welcome to the launch of my new series, The Alpha Brotherhood. Some characters whisper to me as I write. Others boldly shout as I type. However, computer mogul/ Interpol agent Troy Donavan devilishly *winked*.

I adore edgy characters, and exploring the sketchy pasts of The Alpha Brotherhood offers a vast landscape for telling my next Harlequin Desire books. These men have a Robin Hood sense of justice that leads them each to a no-holds-barred life…and love.

And so The Alpha Brotherhood begins with *An Inconvenient Affair.* From Chicago to Costa Rica, I hope you enjoy Troy and Hillary's passionate adventures!

Cheers,

Catherine Mann

Website: www.CatherineMann.com

Facebook: www.facebook.com/CatherineMannAuthor

Twitter: twitter.com/#!/CatherineMann1

CATHERINE MANN

AN INCONVENIENT AFFAIR

HARLEQUIN®
entertain, enrich, inspire™

Recycling programs
for this product may
not exist in your area.

ISBN-13: 978-0-373-73186-2

AN INCONVENIENT AFFAIR

Copyright © 2012 by Catherine Mann

This edition published by arrangement with Harlequin Books S.A.

For questions and comments about the quality of this book please contact us at Customer_eCare@Harlequin.ca.

www.Harlequin.com

Printed in U.S.A.

Other titles by this author available in ebook format.

CATHERINE MANN

USA TODAY bestselling author Catherine Mann lives on a sunny Florida beach with her flyboy husband and their four children. With more than forty books in print in over twenty countries, she has also celebrated wins for both a RITA® Award and a Booksellers' Best Award. Catherine enjoys chatting with readers online—thanks to the wonders of the Internet, which allows her to network with her laptop by the water! Contact Catherine through her website, www.catherinemann.com, on Facebook as Catherine Mann (author), on Twitter as CatherineMann1, or reach her by snail mail at P.O. Box 6065, Navarre, FL 32566.

To my stellar editor, Stacy Boyd! Thank you for the wonderful brainstorming session that gave birth to The Alpha Brotherhood. It's a joy working with you.

Prologue

They'd shaved his head and sent him to a reform school.

Could life suck any worse? Probably. Since he was only fifteen, he had years under the system's thumb to find out.

Hanging around in the doorway to the barracks, Troy Donavan scanned the room for his rack. The dozen bunk beds were half-full of guys with heads shaved as buzz-short as his—another victory for dear old dad, getting rid of his son's long hair. God forbid anyone embarrass the almighty Dr. Donavan. Although, catching the illustrious doc's son breaking into the Department of Defense's computer system did take public embarrassment to a whole new level.

Now he'd been shuttled off to this "jail," politely disguised as a military boarding preparatory program in the hills of North Carolina, as per his plea agreement with the judge back home in Virginia. A judge his father had bought off. Troy clenched his hand around his duffel as he resisted the urge to put his fist through a window just to get some air.

Damn it, he was proud of what he'd done. He didn't want it swept under the rug, and he didn't want to be hidden like some bad secret. If the decision had been left up to him, he would have gone to juvie, or prison even. But for his mom, he'd taken the deal. He would finish high school in this uptight place, but if he kept his grades up and his nose clean until he turned twenty-one, he could have his life back.

He just had to survive living here without his head exploding.

Bunk by bunk, he walked to the last row where he found *Donavan, T. E.* printed on a label attached to the foot of the bed. He slung his duffel bag of boring crap onto the empty bottom bed.

A foot in a spit-shined shoe swung off the top bunk, lazing. "So you're the Robin Hood Hacker." A sarcastic voice drifted down. "Welcome to hell."

Great. "Thanks, and don't call me that."

He hated the whole Robin Hood Hacker headline that had blazed through the news when the story first broke. It made what he did sound like a kid's fairy tale. Which was probably more of his dad's influence, downplaying how his teenage son had exposed corrupt crap that the government had been covering up.

"Don't call you that…or what?" asked the smart-ass on the top bunk with a tag that read: *Hughes, C. T.* "You'll steal my identity and wreck my credit, computer boy?"

Troy rocked back on his heels to check the top bunk and make sure he didn't have the spawn of Satan sleeping above him. If so, the devil wore glasses and read the *Wall Street Journal.*

"Apparently you don't know who I am." With a snap of the page, Hughes ducked back behind his paper. "Loser."

Loser?

Screw that. Troy was a freakin' genius, straight As, already aced the ACT and SAT. Not that his parents seemed to notice or give a damn. His older brother was the real loser—smoking weed, failing out of his second college, knocking up cheerleaders. But their old man considered those forgivable offenses. Problems one's money could easily sweep under the rug.

Getting caught using illegal means to expose corrupt DOD contractors and a couple of congressmen was a little tougher to hide. Therefore, *Troy* had committed the unforgivable crime—making mommy and daddy look bad in front of their friends. Which had been his intent at the start, a lame attempt to get his parents' attention. But once he'd realized what he'd stumbled into—the graft, the bribes, the corruption—the puzzle solver inside him hadn't been able to stop until he'd uncovered it all.

No matter how you looked at it, he hadn't been some Robin Hood do-gooder, damn it.

He yanked open his duffel bag full of uniforms and underwear, trying to keep his eyes off the small mirror on his locker. His shaved head might reflect the light and blind him. And since rumor had it half the guys here had also struck deals, he needed to watch his back and recon until he figured out what each of them had done to land here.

If only he had his computer. He wasn't so good at face-to-face reads. The court-appointed shrink that evaluated him for trial said he had trouble connecting with people and lost himself in the cyberworld as a replacement. The Freud wannabe had been right.

And now he was stuck in a freaking barracks full of people. Definitely his idea of hell.

He hadn't even been able to access a computer to research the criminal losers stuck here with him. Thanks to the judge, he was limited to supervised use of the internet for schoolwork only—in spite of the fact he could handle the academics with his eyes closed.

Boring.

He dropped down to sit beside his bag. There had to be a way out of this place. The swinging foot slowed and a hand slid down.

Mr. Wall Street Journal held a portable video game.

It wasn't a computer, but thank God it was electronic. Something to calm the part of him that was totally freaking over being unplugged. Troy didn't even have to think twice. He palmed the game and kicked back in his bunk. Mr. Wall Street Hughes stayed quiet, no gloating. The guy might actually be legit. No agenda.

For now, Troy had found a way through the monotony. Not just because of the video game. But because there was someone else not all wrapped up tight in the rules.

Maybe his fellow juvie refugees might turn out to be not so bad after all. And if he was wrong—his thumbs flew across the keyboard, blasting through to the next level—at least he had a distraction from his first day in hell.

One

Hillary Wright seriously needed a distraction during her flight from D.C. to Chicago. But not if it meant sitting behind a newlywed couple intent on joining the Mile High Club.

Her cheeks puffed with a big blast of recycled air as she dropped into her window seat and made fast work of hooking up the headset. She would have preferred to watch a movie or even sitcom reruns, but that would mean keeping her eyes open with the risk of seeing the duo in front of her making out under a blanket. She just wanted to get to Chicago, where she could finally put the worst mistake of her life behind her.

Hillary switched from the best of Kenny G before it put her to sleep, clicking through the stations until she settled on a Broadway channel piping in "The Sound of

Music." Passengers pushed down the aisle, a family with a baby and a toddler, then a handful of businessmen and women, all moving past her to the cheap seats where she usually sat. But not today. Today, her first-class seat had been purchased for her by the CIA. And how crazy was that? Until this month, her knowledge of the CIA only came from television shows. Now she had to help them in order to clear her name and stay out of jail.

A moan drifted from the brand-new Mrs. Somebody in front of her.

Oh God, Hillary sagged back into her seat, covering her eyes with her arm. She was so nervous she couldn't even enjoy her first visit to Chicago. She'd dreamed about getting out of her small Vermont hometown. Her job as an event planner in D.C. had seemed like a godsend at first. She met the exciting people she would have only read about in the news otherwise—politicians, movie stars, even royalty.

She'd been starstruck by her wealthy boyfriend's lifestyle. Stupidly so. Until she allowed herself to be blinded to Barry's real intentions in managing philanthropic donations, his lack of a moral compass.

Now she had to dig herself out from under the mess she'd made of her life by trusting the wrong guy, by believing his do-gooder act of tricking rich associates into donating large sums of money to bogus charities, then funneling the money overseas into a Swiss bank account. She'd proven herself to be every bit the gullible, smalltown girl she'd wanted to leave behind.

As of today, her blinders were off.

A flash of skin and pink bra showed between the seats.

She squeezed her eyes shut and lost herself in the do-re-mi refrain even as people bumped past. *Focus. Will away the nerves. Get through the weekend.*

She would identify her scumbag ex-boyfriend's crooked banking acquaintance at the Chicago shindig. Give her official statement to Interpol so they could stop the international money-laundering scheme. Then she could have her life back and save her job.

Once she was back in her boss's good graces, she would again be throwing the kinds of parties she'd wanted to oversee when she'd first become an event planner. Her career would skyrocket with her parties featured in the social section of all major newspapers. Her loser ex would read about her in tabloid magazines in prison and realize how she'd moved on, baby. Maybe she would even appear in some of those photos looking so damn hot Barry would suffer in his celibate cell.

The jackass.

She pinched the bridge of her nose against the welling of tears.

A tap on her shoulder forced her out of her silly self-pity. She tugged off an earbud and looked over at a…suit. A dark blue suit, with a Hugo Boss tie and a vintage tie clip.

"Excuse me, ma'am. You're in my seat."

A low voice, nice, and not cranky-sounding like some travelers could be. His face was shadowed, the sunlight streaking through the small window behind him. She could just make out his dark brown hair, which was long enough to brush his ears and the top of his collar. From the Patek Philippe watch to his edgy Caraceni suit—all name brands she wouldn't have heard of, much less recognized, before her work with high-end D.C. clients.

And she *was* in his seat.

Wincing, she pretended to look at her ticket even though she already knew what it read. God, she hated the aisle and she'd prayed she would luck out and have an empty next to her. "I'm sorry. You're right."

"You know what?" He rested a hand on the back of the empty seat. "If you prefer the window, that's cool by me. I'll sit here instead."

"I don't want to take advantage." Take advantage? The cheesy double entendre made her wince. A moan from the lovebirds a row ahead only made it worse.

"No worries." He stowed his briefcase in the overhead before sidling in to sit down.

Then he turned to her, the light above bringing him fully into focus— And holy cows on her hometown Vermont farm, he was *hot*. Angular. But with long lashes that kept drawing her gaze back to his green eyes. He was probably in his early thirties, gauging from the creases when he smiled with the open kind of grin that made him more approachable.

She tilted her head to the side, studying him more closely. He looked familiar, but she couldn't quite place him.... She shook off the feeling. She'd met so many people at the parties she'd planned in D.C. They could have crossed paths at any number of places. Although, she must have seen him from a distance, because if they'd met up close, she definitely wouldn't have forgotten him.

His seat belt clicked as the plane began taxiing. "You don't like flying."

"Why do you say that?"

"You want the window seat, but have the shade closed. You've already plugged into the radio. And you've got the armrest in a death grip."

Handsome and observant. Hmm...

Better to claim fear of flying than to go into the whole embarrassing mess she'd made of her life. "Busted. You caught me." She nodded toward the row in front of her just as one of the seats reclined providing too clear a view of a man's hand sliding into the woman's waistband. "And the lovebirds up there aren't making things any more comfortable."

His smile faded into a scowl. "I'll call for the flight attendant."

He reached for the button overhead. She touched his wrist. Static snapped. At least she hoped it was just static and not a spark of attraction.

Clearing her throat, she folded her arms over her chest, tucking her hands away. "No need. The flight attendant's in the middle of her in-flight brief—" she lowered her voice "—and giving us the death glare for talking."

He leaned toward her conspiratorially. "Or I can kick the back of their seat until they realize they're not invisible—and that they're being damned inconsiderate."

Except now that he was so close, she didn't notice them. Her gaze locked on the glinting green eyes staring at her with undisguised, unrepentant interest.

A salve to her ego. And an excellent distraction. "I guess we can live and let live."

"We can."

"Although, honestly, it doesn't seem fair the flight attendant isn't giving the evil eye to the handsy twosome."

"Maybe they're celebrating their anniversary."

She snorted.

"Cynic?"

"And you're trying to tell me you're a true believer in flowery romance?" She took in his expensive suit, his dimpled smile and his easy charm. "No offense, truly, but you seem more like a player to me."

A second after the words left her mouth, she worried she might have been rude.

He just laughed softly and flattened a hand to his chest.

"You think the worst of me. I'm hurt to the core," he said with overplayed drama.

Her snort turned into a laugh. Shaking her head, she kept on laughing, tension uncurling inside. Her laughter faded as she felt the weight of his gaze on her.

He pointed to the window. "We're airborne now. You can open the shade and relax."

Relax? His words confused her for a second and then she remembered her excuse for nerves. And then remembered the real reason for her nerves. Her ex-boyfriend. Barry the Bastard Bum. Who she was hoping to help put in prison once she identified his accomplice in Chicago— if she didn't get offed by the bad guy first.

She thumbed her silver seat belt buckle. "Thank you for the help…"

"Troy." He extended his hand. "My name is Troy, from Virginia."

"I'm Hillary, from D.C." Prepping herself for the static this time, she wrapped her fingers around his, shaking once. And, yep. *Snap. Snap.* Heat tingled up her arm in spite of all those good intentions to keep all guys at bay. But then what was wrong with simply being attracted to another person?

Her ex had taken so much from her, and yes, turned a farm-fresh girl like her into a cynic, making her doubt everyone around her. Until she now questioned the motives of a guy who just wanted to indulge in a little harmless flirtation on a plane.

Damn it, there was nothing bad about chatting with this guy during the flight. He had helped her through her nerves about identifying Barry's accomplice at the fundraiser this weekend. A very slippery accomplice who had a way of avoiding cameras. Very few people had ever seen him. She'd only seen him twice, once by showing up at

Barry's condo unannounced and another time at Barry's office. Would the man remember her? Her nerves doubled.

She desperately needed to take full advantage of the distraction this man beside her offered. Talking to Troy beat the hell out of getting sloshed off the drink cart, especially since she didn't even drink.

"So, Troy, what's taking you to Chicago?"

Troy had recognized Hillary Wright the minute he'd stepped on the plane. She looked just like her Interpol file photo, right down to the freckles on her nose and the natural sun streaks through her red hair.

The photo hadn't, however, shown anything below the neck—a regrettable oversight because she was…hot. Leggy with curves and an unadorned innocence that normally wasn't his type. But then when had he ever given a crap about walking the expected path?

That's why he'd shown up here, on her flight, rather than following the plan laid out by the CIA operatives, who were working in conjunction with the American branch of Interpol. To see what she was like in an unguarded moment.

Lucky for him that window seat was empty so he'd been able to wrangle his way in beside her. It had been too easy, and she was totally unsuspecting. She might as well have "fresh off the farm" tattooed across her freckled nose.

A sexy uptipped nose he wouldn't mind kissing as he worked his way around to her ear. He'd expected pretty from her picture, but he hadn't been prepared for the undefinable energy that radiated off her. It was as damn near tangible as her innocence.

This plane on the way to Chicago was the last place she should be. More so, that viper's nest gala this weekend was *absolutely* the last place she should be.

Damn, damn, damn the "powers that be" for making her a part of some crazy power play. He could have accomplished the identification in Chicago without her, but they'd insisted on having her backup confirmation. It was obvious to him now that she was too naive to brush elbows with the sharks at that gala—a bunch of crooks using a fundraiser to cover up their international money laundering.

"Troy? Hello?" Hillary waved her hand in front of his face, her nails chewed to the quick. "What takes you to Chicago?"

"Business trip." Truth. "I'm in computers." More truth. Enough for now. She would see him again soon enough after they landed and when she learned who he really was... Well, she would likely change, close up or suck up. People judged him based on either his past or his money. "What takes *you* to Chicago?" he asked, even though he already knew.

"A fundraiser gala. I'm an event planner and, uhm, my boss is sending me to check out a chef at this weekend retreat."

She was a really crummy liar. Even if he didn't already know her real reason for going to Chicago, he would have sensed something was off in her story.

"A chef... In Chicago... And you work in D.C. You work for lobbyists?"

"I specialize in fundraisers for charities, not campaigns. I didn't plan the one in Chicago. I'm just, uh, scoping out competition. It's a pretty big deal, kicking off Friday night, running all the way to Sunday afternoon with parties and—" She paused self-consciously. "I'm babbling. You don't need the agenda."

"You specialize in polishing the halos of the rich and famous." He smiled on the outside.

Her lips pursed tightly. "Think what you want. I don't need your approval."

A sentiment he applauded. So why was he yanking her chain? Because she looked so damn pretty with righteous indignation sparking from her eyes.

That kind of "in your face" mentality was rare. But it also could land a person in trouble.

He knew too well. It had taken all his self-control to buckle down and meet the judge's requirements when he'd been sentenced at fifteen. Although, he'd found more than he expected at the military school. He'd found friends and a new code to live by. He'd learned how to play by the rules. He'd slowly gotten back computer access and started a video games company that had him rolling in more money than his pedigreed, doctor old man had ever brought home—three times over.

But the access had come with a price. His every move had been monitored by the FBI. They seemed to sense that the taste of megapower he'd felt delving into the DOD would be addictive. Irresistibly so. At twenty-one, he'd been approached with an enticing offer. If he ever wanted a chance at that high again, he would need to loan his "skills" to the American branch of Interpol on occasion.

He'd chafed at the idea at twenty-one. By thirty-two, he'd come to begrudgingly accept that he had to play by a few of their rules, and he'd even found a rush in being a sort of "on call" guy to assist in major international sting operations. He was committed to the job, as he'd proven every time they'd tapped him for a new assignment.

Over time, they also began utilizing him for more than computer help. His wealth gave him access to high-power circles. When Interpol needed a contact on the inside quickly, they used him—and other freelance agents like him. For the most part, he still provided behind-the-scenes computer advice. He was only called upon for something out in the open like this about once a year, so as not to overuse his cover.

Some of that caution would have been nice now, rather than recklessly including Hillary Wright in this joint operation being run by the CIA and Interpol. She wouldn't be able to carry off the charade this weekend. She couldn't blend in.

He'd known it the second he read her profile, even if they'd missed it. God only knew why they called him a genius and then refused to listen to him. So he'd arranged to meet her on this flight to confirm his suspicions. He was never wrong. He would stick by her side all weekend and make sure she didn't blow the whole operation.

Granted, that wouldn't be a hardship, sticking near her for the weekend.

For the first time in years he wasn't bored. Something about this woman intrigued him, and there weren't many puzzles in life for him. So he would stay right here for the rest of the flight and play this through. When she found out his full name—his public, infamous identity—she would pull away. She would likely never know his real reason for being part of this sting, and someone like Hillary Wright wouldn't go for a guy with the reputation of Troy Donavan, especially so soon after getting her fingers burned in the relationship department.

Not that he would let that affect his decision to stick by her. She needed him to get through this weekend, whether she knew it or not.

A flight attendant ducked to ask, "Could I get either of you a complimentary beverage? Wine? A mixed drink?"

Hillary's smile froze, the lightheartedness fading from

her face with the one simple request. The mention of alcohol stirred painful memories. "No, thank you.

Troy shook his head. "I'm good. Thanks." He turned back to Hillary. "Are you sure you don't want a glass of wine or something? A lot of folks drink to get over the fear."

She inched away from the wall and sat upright self-consciously. "I don't drink."

"Ever?"

She refused to risk ending up like her mother, in and out of alcohol rehabs every other year while her father continued to hold out hope that this time, the program would stick. It never did.

There was nothing for her at home. D.C. was her chance at a real life. She couldn't let anything risk ruining this opportunity. Not a drink. Not some charming guy, either.

"Never," she answered. "I never drink."

"There's a story there." He toyed with his platinum cuff links.

"There is." And honest to God, the bay rum scent of him was intoxicating enough.

"But you're not sharing."

"Not with a total stranger." She was an expert at keeping family secrets, of sweeping up the mess so they would look normal to the outside world. Planning high-profile galas for the D.C. elite was a piece of cake after keeping up appearances as a teenager.

She might look like a naive farm girl, but life had already done its fair share to leave her jaded. Which might be why she found herself questioning the ease of her past hour with Troy.

Nothing about him was what she'd expected once he'd first flashed that bad-boy grin in her direction. They'd spent the entire flight just...talking. They'd discussed favorite artists and foods. Found they both liked jazz music and hokey horror movies. He was surprisingly well-read, could quote Shakespeare and had a sharp sense of humor. There was interest in his eyes, but his words stayed light all the way to the start of the plane's descent.

His eyes narrowed at her silence. "Is something wrong?"

"You're not hitting on me," she blurted out.

He blinked in surprise just once before that wicked slow smile spread across his face. "Do you want me to?"

"Actually, I'm having fun just like this."

She sat back and waited for him to stop grinning when he realized she wasn't coming on to him. Was she? She never went for this kind of guy, hair too long and a couple of tiny scars on his face like he was always getting into some kind of trouble. A line through one eyebrow. Another on his chin. And yet another on his forehead that played peekaboo when his hair shifted.

But then Barry had been Mr. Buttoned-Up, clean-cut and respectful. Except it had all been a cover for a deceitful nature.

Troy stared deeper into her eyes. "You don't get to have fun often, do you?"

Who had time for fun? She'd worked hard these past three years building a new life for herself, far away from a gossipy small town that knew her as the daughter of a drunk mother. Barry had tarnished her reputation with his shady dealings—stealing scholarship money for God's sake. And unless she proved otherwise, people would always think she was involved, as well. They wouldn't trust her.

Her boss wouldn't trust her.

She picked at the hem of her skirt. "Why would you say I'm a wet blanket?"

"Not a wet blanket. Just a workaholic. The portfolio under your seat is stuffed with official-looking papers, rather than a book or magazine. The chewed-down nails on your otherwise beautiful hands—sure shout stress."

She'd tried balancing her career and a relationship. That hadn't gone very well for her. Thank you very much, Barry, for being a white-collar crook—and not even all that good of an embezzler, given how easily he'd been caught. She'd been so busy with her job that she'd completely missed the signs that he'd been using her to get close to her clients—and sucker them in.

"Troy, I'm simply devoted to my career." Which would be wrecked if she didn't make sure everyone knew she was a hundred percent against what Barry had done. Her boss would fire her and no one else would hire her since the clients would never trust her. "Aren't you?"

What exactly did he do in computers? She was just beginning to realize that they'd talked all about her and not so much about him and the flight was already almost over.

"Work rocks—as do vacations. So if you were taking this plane trip for pleasure, no work worries and you could pick up any connecting flight when we touch down—where would you go?"

"Overseas." She answered fast before realizing that again, he'd turned the conversation away from himself.

"That's a broad choice," he said as the ground grew larger and larger, downtown Chicago coming into focus.

"I would close my eyes and pick, some place far away." Far, far away from the Windy City gala.

"Ah, the old escape idea. I get that, totally. When I was in boarding school, I made plans for places to live and visit, places without fences."

Boarding school? Interesting and so far removed from her childhood riding the ancient bus with cracked leather seats each morning with all the friends from her neighborhood.

She settled deeper into her seat. "Isn't that the whole point of a vacation? To do something that is totally the opposite of your daily routine. Like open spaces being different from the walls of your old boarding school."

"You have a point." His smile went tight for a flash before his face cleared. "Where are you from originally—so I can get a sense of your daily routine when I'm choosing our great escape?"

Our? "Theoretically of course."

"Theoretically? Nu-uh. You're wrecking the fantasy."

"Right, sorry about that." His magnetism had a way of drawing her into this fantasy. No harm in that. "I'm from Vermont, a tiny town nobody's heard of. Coming to D.C. was a big enough change for me—and now I'm going to Chicago."

"But you don't look happy about it."

She forced herself not to flinch. He was too perceptive. Time to put some distance between them, let him show himself to be a jerk so she could move on. "I'm scared of flying, remember? And this is where you're supposed to ask me for my phone number."

"Would you give it to me if I did?"

"No," she said, almost believing what she was saying. "I'm not in a good place to date anyone right now. So you can stop trying to charm me."

"Can't a guy be nice without wanting something other than engaging conversation?"

She couldn't help but smile. "Did you really just say that?"

He slumped back in his seat, respect glinting in his eyes. "Okay, you're right. I would like to ask for your phone number—because I am single, in case you were wondering—but since you've made it clear you're not open to my advances, I'll satisfy my broken heart and soothe my wounded ego with the pleasure of your company for a little while longer."

God, he was good. Funny and charming, so confident he didn't think twice about making a joke at his own expense. "Do you practice lines like that or are you just really good at improvisation?"

"You're a smart woman. I'm confident you'll figure it out."

She liked him. Damn it. "You're funny."

"And you are enchanting. It was my pleasure to sit next to you on the flight."

They'd landed? She looked around as if waking up from a nap to find more time had passed than she realized. Passengers were sliding from their seats. The aircraft had stopped.

Troy stood, hauling her simple black roll bag from the overhead. "Yours?"

"How did you know?"

He tapped the little dairy cow name tag attached to the handle. "Vermont. Highest cows to people ratio in the country."

"Right you are." She stood, stopping beside him. Close beside him. All the other passengers crowded the aisle until her breasts brushed his chest.

His rock-hard chest. That suit covered one hundred percent honed man, whipcord lean. The bay rum scent of him wrapping around her completely now, rather than just teasing—tempting—her senses.

But still, he didn't touch her or hit on her or act in the least bit skeezy. "Have a great visit in the Windy City."

She chewed her bottom lip, resisting the overwhelming urge to tug his silk tie.

The flight attendant spoke over the loudspeaker. "If you could please return to your seats. We have a slight delay before we can disembark at the gate."

Hillary pulled away quickly, ducking into her seat so fast she almost hit her head. Troy reclaimed his seat slowly while the flight attendant opened the hatch. The yawning opening revealed the long metal stairs that had been rolled up outside. Confused, Hillary yanked up her window shade. They'd stopped just shy of the terminal. A large black SUV with some kind of official insignia on the door waited a few feet away. Two men wearing black suits and sunglasses jogged up the stairs and entered the plane.

The first one nodded to the flight attendant. "Thank you, ma'am. We'll be quick with our business."

The identical duo angled sideways.

Her stomach tumbled over itself. Was there a problem? In spite of what she'd told Troy, she hadn't been freaked out about flying, but now she felt that lie come back to bite her as fears fluttered inside her. How long before she knew what was wr—

Not long at all, apparently.

The dark-suited men stopped beside her row. "Troy Donavan?"

Troy Donavan?

Her stomach lurched faster than a major turbulence plunge. Oh God, she recognized that name. She waited for him to deny it…even though she already knew he wouldn't.

"Yes, that's me. Is there a problem, gentlemen?"

Troy Donavan.

He'd confirmed it. He was far from a nice guy, far from some computer geek just passing time on a commuter flight. His reputation for partying hard and living on the edge made it into the social pages on a regular basis.

"Mr. Donavan, would you step out of your seat, please?"

Troy shot an apologetic look her way before he angled out to stand in front of the two men. "We could have met up at the gate like regular folks."

The older man, the guy who seemed in charge, shook his head. "It's better this way. We don't want to keep Colonel Salvatore waiting."

"Of course. Can't inconvenience the colonel." Muscles bunched in Troy's arms, his hands fisting at his sides.

What the hell was going on?

The "men in black" retrieved Troy's Italian leather briefcase and placed a streamlined linen fedora on his head, the same look that had been featured in countless articles. If she'd seen him in his signature hat, she would have recognized him in a heartbeat.

He was infamous in D.C. for having hacked the Department of Defense's computer system seventeen years ago. She'd been all of ten at the time but he'd become an icon. From then on, any computer hacking was called "pulling a Donavan." He'd made it into pop culture lexicons. He'd become a folk legend for the way he'd leaked information that exposed graft and weaknesses within the system. Some argued he'd merely stepped in where authorities and politicians should have. But there was no denying he'd broken major laws. If he'd been an adult, he would have spent his life in jail.

After a slap-on-the-wrist sentence in some military school, he'd been free to make billions and live out his life in a totally decadent swirl of travel and conspicuous consumption. And she'd fallen for his lying charm. She'd even liked him. She hadn't learned a damn thing from Barry.

She bit her lip against the disappointment in herself. She was here to put the past behind her—not complicate her future. She pressed her back against the body of the plane, unable to get far enough away from the man who'd charmed the good sense right out of her.

Troy reached for his briefcase, but the younger man took a step back.

The older of the two men held out...*handcuffs*.

Cocking an eyebrow, Troy said, "Are these really needed?"

"I'm afraid they are." *Click. Click.* "Troy Donavan, you're under arrest."

Two

"Were the handcuffs necessary?" Holding up his shackled hands, Troy sprawled in the backseat of the armored SUV as they powered away from the airport. The duo that had arrested him sat in the front. His mentor and former military school headmaster—Colonel John Salvatore—sat beside him with a smirk on his face.

As always, he wore a gray suit and red tie, no variation, same thing every day as if wearing a uniform even though he'd long ago left the army.

"Yes, Troy, actually they are required, as per the demands of the grand dame throwing this gala. She's determined to have a bachelor auction like one she read about in a romance novel and she thought, given your checkered past, the handcuffs would generate buzz. And honest to God, the photos in the paper will only help your image, and therefore our purposes, as well."

It was always about their purposes. Their agreement.

He'd struck a deal with Colonel Salvatore at twenty-one years old, once his official sentence was complete. Salvatore had been the headmaster of that military reform school—and more. Apparently he helped recruit freelancers for Interpol who could assist with difficult assignments—such as using Troy's computer skills and later utilizing his access to high-power circles. Other graduates of the military school had been recruited, as well, people who could use their overprivileged existence to quickly move in high-profile circles. For these freelancers, no setup was needed for a cover story, a huge time and money saver for the government.

A person might be called on once. Or once a year. Maybe more. Salvatore offered things no one else in Troy's life had ever given him. A real chance to atone.

He may not have felt guilty at fifteen, but over time he'd come to realize the repercussions of what he'd done were far-reaching. His big DOD computer exposé as a teen had inadvertently exposed two undercover operatives. And even though they hadn't died, their careers had been cut short, their usefulness in the field ruined.

He should have taken his information to the authorities rather than giving it to the press. He'd been full of ego and the need to piss off his father. He knew better now, and had the opportunity to make up for what he'd cost the government and those two agents.

And yeah, he still enjoyed the rush of flying close to the flame while doing it.

Troy worked his hands inside the cuffs. "You could have waited. There was no need to freak out Hillary Wright. I would think you'd want her calm."

Her horrified, disillusioned blue eyes were burned in his memory as deeply as the sound of her laugh and the genuine warmth of her smile.

Sighing, Salvatore swiped a hand over his closely shorn head. "If you'd been on the private jet like you were supposed to be none of this would have happened. Stop caring what Hillary Wright thinks of you. She'll be out of your life by Monday. Your time will be your own soon enough and, with luck, I won't need to call on you again for a long while."

The years stretched ahead in monotony. His company all but ran itself now. The past eleven months since he'd been called upon had been boring as hell.

His mind zipped back to Hillary and how he would see her for the rest of the weekend—how she would see him. "A bachelor auction, huh? That grand dame can't expect me to strut down some catwalk."

"When did *you* start worrying about appearances?"

"When did *you* start using innocents like Hillary?" he snapped back, unsettled by the protective surge pumping through him. At least he would have a chance to explain to her some of what had happened on the plane. He could claim the event swore him to secrecy about the handcuffing gig, even if he wasn't authorized to tell her about his role with Interpol. "I thought your gig was to, uh, collaborate with the fallen."

"My 'gig' is to mentor people with potential. Always has been."

"Mentor. Jailer."

Salvatore smirked. "Someone's grouchy."

Troy rattled his cuffs as they drove deeper into the skyscraper-filled city. "Could you just take the cuffs off?"

He hated being confined and Salvatore knew that, damn it. Although looking at the cuffs now, other uses scrolled through his head, sexy fantasies of using them with Hillary. Maybe he would lock his wrist to hers, and take it from there.

"The mistress of ceremonies has the key."

"You're joking." He had to be. "That's hours away."

"When have I ever had a sense of humor?"

"Valid point." Troy's hands fell in his lap. He might as well settle in for the scenic ride through downtown Chicago. He would be free, eventually, and then he would check on Hillary. For now, he was stuck with Salvatore.

The colonel was one eccentric dude.

Sure, Salvatore was the Interpol handler for the group of freelancers whose lifestyles gave them a speedy entrée into a high-profile circle when fast action was needed. But it must blow to be an overgrown babysitter for Troy at some shindig hosted by a local grand dame at a downtown hotel. Tonight's gala kicked off a whole weekend of partying for the rich and famous, under the pretense of charity work.

And apparently Salvatore wasn't just here for Troy, but helping the CIA by being here for Hillary, too.

"Colonel, I am curious, though, why do we need Hillary for this? How much does she know?"

The more Troy learned about her, the more of an edge he would have over her the next time he saw her.

"She's here to identify contacts of her former boyfriend. And because we and the CIA need to be sure she's truly as innocent as she seems."

Was his protectiveness misplaced? Could he have so misread her? Either way, it didn't dim how damn badly he wanted to peel her power suit off with his teeth. "This is really just to test her?"

The colonel waved aside Troy's indignation. "Speaking of Hillary Wright. Your little stunt—switching from the private jet to her flight? Not cool. I had to cancel lunch with an ambassador to get here in time."

"You're breaking my heart."

Sighing, Salvatore shook his head. "How the hell did you even get on that plane?"

"Really?" Troy cocked an eyebrow. "Do you even have to ask *me,* the guy who broke through the school's supposedly impenetrable computer firewalls in order to hack your bank account and send flowers to the Latin teacher on your behalf?"

A laugh rumbled in the old guy's chest. "As I recall, that trick didn't go so well for you since she and I were quietly seeing each other and I'd already sent her flowers. She figured out fast who pulled that off."

"But the flowers I chose were better—Casablanca lilies, if I recall."

"And I learned from that. Same way you should accept you can learn from others once in a while." Salvatore and the teacher had eventually married—and divorced. The man's laughter faded into a scowl. "The internet is not your personal plaything."

Troy held up his cuffed wrists. "These give me hives *and* flashbacks."

Salvatore's eyes narrowed. "I don't know why I put up with you."

"Because I'll get the job done. I always do. I'll find our mystery guy either in person or through the hotel's security system. I will make sure this time that he doesn't get away with hiding from the cameras. We will track his accounts and nail the bastard." He'd only caught a glimpse of the guy once, a month ago shortly before they'd taken down Barry Curtis. If only they'd caught both men then… "But now, as far as I'm concerned, my job also includes making sure Hillary Wright stays safe in that pool of piranhas posing as scions of society."

"As long as you don't make a spectacle of yourself or her, I can live with that. Keep it low-key for once."

"Okay, deal," he agreed, perhaps a bit too quickly because Salvatore's eyes narrowed suspiciously. Time for a diversion. "One last thing, though."

"You're pushy today."

"Look in my briefcase. I brought John Junior—" Salvatore's only kid "—a copy of Alpha Realms IV. He'll have a month's head start mastering it before it hits the market."

"Bribery's a crime." But Salvatore still reached for the Italian leather case. "What's the favor?"

"It's just a gift for your son from my software company. No strings attached."

"What's the favor?" he repeated.

"I don't agree with your pulling Hillary Wright into this. She's too naive and uninformed. After the party tonight, I want her sent home to D.C. Scrap keeping her around for the weekend."

Troy would figure out a way to contact her in D.C., without all the hidden agenda crap. But make no mistake, he would see her again.

"She's not so innocent if she was involved with Barry Curtis." The colonel slid the video game into his black briefcase. "She'll prove herself this weekend—or not."

"Guilty of bad judgment, that's all." Troy was sure of that. What he didn't know—something that bothered him even more—was if Hillary still had feelings for the creep.

God, why did he feel such a connection to a woman he'd only just met? Maybe because she possessed an innocence he'd never had.

"Are you so sure about her?" The leather seats creaked as Salvatore shifted back into place.

Troy was certain he couldn't let her go into a ballroom full of crooks alone. "I'm sticking with her tonight and putting her on a plane in the morning."

Salvatore patted his briefcase. "You should really keep

me happy if you want me to put in a good word with your brother's parole officer."

Troy looked up sharply. Pulling in his brother was dirty pool, even for Salvatore.

"I'm not an enabler." His brother, Devon, had more than a drug problem. He'd blown through his trust fund and had been sent to jail for dealing to feed his cocaine addiction. Troy forced himself to say blandly, "Do whatever you want with him."

"Tough love or sibling rivalry?"

Anger pulsed—at Salvatore for jabbing at old wounds. "You'd better tell the driver to move this along so I can get out of these handcuffs before I have to take a leak. Otherwise you'll have to help."

"Bathroom humor is beneath you, Donavan."

"I wasn't joking." He pinned Salvatore with an impassive look as the SUV stopped in front of the towering hotel.

Salvatore reached for the door handle as the driver opened Troy's side. "Time to rock and roll."

Standing in the elevator in the Chicago hotel, Hillary smoothed her sweaty palms down the length of her simple black dress. Strapless and floor length, it was her favorite. She'd brought it, along with her good luck charm clipped to her clutch purse, to bolster her and steady her nerves. It wasn't working. Her hands went nervously to her hair, which was straight with a simple crystal clasp sweeping back one side.

She'd been nervous enough about this weekend from the moment she'd been asked to come to Chicago, but at least she'd had a plan. She'd thought she had her head on straight—and then she'd fallen right into flirting with a notorious guy seconds away from handcuffs. The experience had thrown her. Right now, she wasn't sure of much of anything.

There'd been a time, as a little girl, when she'd dreamed of staying in a five-star hotel like this one, in a big city, with all the glitz included. As a kid, after she'd finished her chores on the dairy farm, she'd hidden in her room, away from her drunken mother. For hours and hours, Hillary had played on the internet, escaping into another world. Researching other places and other ways to live. Clean places. Pretty, even.

With tables full of food.

She'd spent a lot of time thinking about the cuisine, learning recipes, planning meals and parties to fill her solitary world. Even if only in her imagination.

Once she'd turned eighteen, she scrounged together enough college loans to get a degree in hospitality and economics. Three years ago, she'd landed with a major D.C. corporation that contracted out events planners. Someday, she hoped to start her own company. Be in charge of her own business. She refused to live her life as the scared little country girl she'd once been, hiding in her room, too afraid to slip out and grab a mushy apple from behind mom's beer.

The elevator doors slid open and she smiled her thanks to the attendant before stepping out into the wide hall, sconces lighting the way into the glittering ballroom. Nerves ate at her stomach like battery acid. She just had to get through this weekend. She'd make the proper identifications, which would help confirm her innocence. Or at least get her off the hook, even if they still didn't believe she'd known nothing about what Barry had in mind for those supposed college scholarships.

Forging ahead, she passed her invitation to the tuxedoed man protecting the elite fundraising bash from party crashers. Media cameras flashed. Even with spots in front of her eyes, she already recognized at least two movie stars, an opera singer and three politicians. This party rivaled anything she'd seen or planned—and her standards were top-notch. The ballroom glittered with refracted lights from the crystal chandeliers. Columns and crown molding were gilded; plush carpets held red-and-brass swirls.

A harpist and a violinist played—for now—but from the looks of the instruments set up throughout the room, the music would obviously be staggered. The stage was set for a string quartet. A grand piano filled a corner, with a 1940s-era mic in place alongside.

The dance—at two thousand dollars a head—was slated to fund scholarships. But then that was the root of Barry's scam—collecting money for scholarships, most of which were never awarded, then funneling the cash out of the country into a Swiss bank account.

Bile rose in her throat. She thumbed the charm clipped to her bag, rubbing the tiny silver cow pin like a talisman, a reminder of where she'd come from and all she intended to accomplish.

Men wore tuxedos or military uniforms, the women were in long dresses and dripping jewels that would have funded endless numbers of scholarships. Well, everyone wore formal attire except for the gentleman in a gray suit with a red tie. Her contact.

Colonel Salvatore.

She'd been introduced to him by her lawyer. Apparently, the colonel worked for international authorities. The CIA had promised he would ensure her safety and oversee her cooperation while she was in Chicago. Only one more weekend and she could put this all behind her.

The colonel stepped up beside her and offered his arm.

"Miss Wright, you're here early. I would have escorted you down if I'd known you were ready."

"I couldn't wait any longer to get this evening under way." She tucked her hand into the crook of his arm. "I hope you understand."

"Of course." He started into the ballroom, moving toward the seating section with a runway thrust into the middle.

She recalled there being some mention of an auction of items donated by the elite from around the globe.

More money laundering? Couldn't anyone or anything be genuine anymore? Was everything tainted with greed and agendas?

Salvatore gestured her toward a seat reserved with his name and "guest". They took their places five rows back, not conspicuously in the front. She was also in the perfect spot to see both of the screens panning shots of the guests while a matriarch of Chicago high society took the stage to emcee the auction. Of course Colonel Salvatore had planned everything.

Hillary forced herself to focus on studying each face on the screen, on searching for the two familiar individuals who Barry had claimed were his "silent partners"— not that Barry was talking to authorities now that he'd lawyered up.

But then when had she ever been able to count on a man? Her father certainly hadn't done anything to stop her mother from drinking or to protect Hillary and her sister. He'd buried himself in working in the fields, and as long as she worked alongside him, she was safe.

The hard work of her childhood had taught her to work hard as an adult. Life was just hard. Plain and simple. She was still trying to keep herself safe so her efforts could finally pay off.

As bid after bid went by for posh vacations, jewelry and even private concerts, her thoughts raced back to Troy Donavan and that hour of lighthearted banter on the plane. For a short snap, life had felt fun and uncomplicated.

Yet, it had all been a lie. She couldn't have bantered with a more complicated person. Troy was a perfect example of the cold, hard truth. Everyone wanted something from someone else. People didn't do things exclusively out of the goodness of their hearts. There was always a payoff of some sort expected. The sooner she accepted that and quit believing otherwise, the happier she would be.

Madame Emcee moved closer to the microphone, her gold taffeta dress smooshed against the podium. "And now, before we move on to dancing the night away, we have one final auction left for the evening, one not on your programs." She swept a bejeweled hand toward the large flat screens. "If you'll turn your attention to our video feed, you'll see media footage you may have caught earlier."

Troy Donavan's face filled the screen.

Oh. God.

Hillary clenched her hands around her handbag, the silver charm cutting into her palm. She glanced quickly at the colonel to see if he'd noticed her panic. But her escort simply sat with his arms folded, watching along with everyone else.

In full color, high-definition, the whole runway scenario played out again in front of her. Troy, walking off the plane in handcuffs, wearing that quirky, undeniably sexy hat. Troy, escorted into some official-looking SUV. Hillary had been so rushed getting checked in and ready for the kickoff gala, she hadn't even turned on the television in her room.

Madame Emcee continued, "But what does that have to do with us tonight? Prepare yourself."

The lights shut off. The ballroom went pitch-black. Gasps rippled. A woman squeaked.

After a squeal of microphone feedback, the emcee continued, "For our final bid of the night, we have for you…"

A spotlight illuminated a circle on stage.

Troy Donavan stood in the middle, wearing a tuxedo now instead of his suit, but still cuffed with his hands in front of him. A white silk scarf gave him the same quirky air he'd had on the plane. Her eyes took in the whole man. How could she not? He'd been hot in a suit—in a tuxedo, he stole the air from the room.

"Yes," Madame continued, her fat diamond earrings sparkling disco ball refractions all around her face. "Troy Donavan has offered himself as a date for the weekend. But first, someone must 'bid' him out of our custody in an auction. He's been a bad, bad boy, ladies. You'll want to handle with caution and by no means, let this computer whiz get his hands on your software."

Laughter echoed up into the rafters from everyone— except Hillary. She sat stunned; her hands gripped the sides of her seat so tightly her fingers went numb. The whole arrest had been a gag, a publicity stunt for this party. She'd spent the entire afternoon thinking of him in a jail cell—and yes, sad over that in spite of her anger.

Now she was just mad. He had to have known what she thought in those last minutes on the airplane and he'd said nothing to reassure her. He didn't even bother to lean down and whisper "Sorry" in her ear.

She should be relieved he wasn't in trouble, and she was. But she couldn't forget. He was still the Robin Hood Hacker.

Still playing games.

The bidding began—and of course it soared. Half the women and a couple of men were falling all over themselves to win a weekend with him. The war continued, shouts growing louder and escalating to over seventy thousand dollars. The ruckus continued until just three bidders remained.

Winning at the moment was a woman wearing skin-tight silver and chunky sapphires, with a sheen of plastic surgery to her stretched skin.

Not far behind, a college-aged student who'd begged Daddy for more money twice already.

And coolly chiming in occasionally, a sedate woman in a simple black sheath.

College girl dropped out after her daddy shook his head at the auctioneer and drew his hand across his throat in the universal "cut off" signal. Still the bidding rose another ten thousand dollars, money that would go to underprivileged schoolkids who needed scholarships. This was all in fun, right?

Yet, the way these people tossed around money in games left her...unsettled. Why not just write a check, plus cancel the event and donate that amount, too? Of course if they did that, she would be out of a job.

Who was she to stand in judgment of others? Of Troy?

As much as she wanted to look away from his cocky smile, which had so charmed her earlier, she couldn't. The way she stayed glued to the bidding upset her. A lot.

She found herself rooting for the one less likely to entice him. Not that she really knew anything about him. But a part of her sensed—or hoped—Ms. Plastic Surgery with her wedding ring wouldn't be at all alluring to Troy. And if she was, then how much easier it would be to wipe him from her mind.

But the sedate woman in the black dress? She could have been Hillary's cousin. And that gave her pause. If that woman won and if she was his type, then that meant he could have been genuine on the airplane when he flirted....

As fast as "going, going, gone" echoed through the room, Ms. Sedate had a date with Troy Donavan for the weekend, won by an eighty-nine-thousand-dollar bid. And gauging from his huge "cat ate the canary smile" he was happy with the results.

The depth of Hillary's disappointment was ridiculous, damn it. She'd spoken to the guy for all of an hour on a flight. Yes, she'd been inordinately attracted to him—felt a zap of chemistry she hadn't felt before—but she could chalk that up to her vulnerable state right now. She was raw, with her emotions tender and close to the surface. After this ordeal with Barry was over, she would get stronger.

The emcee moved closer to Troy in a loud crackle of gold taffeta, which carried through the microphone. She keyed open the cuffs and he tucked them into his tuxedo pocket. He kissed her hand before taking the mic from her.

"Ladies and gentlemen," he said in that same carefree voice that had so enticed Hillary earlier as he'd calmed her nerves on the plane, "I'm pleased to be a part of such a generous outpouring tonight—all in the Robin Hood spirit and not a single computer hacked."

There was no denying it. The crowd loved him. They all but ate up his irreverence and charm. All except Colonel Salvatore. He seemed—skeptical.

"As you're all aware, I'm not known for playing by the rules. And tonight's no different." He motioned to the reserved woman who'd won the bidding battle. "My assistant here has been placing bids for me so I'll have the opportunity to pick the lady of my choice for the weekend."

Gasps, whispers and a couple of disgruntled murmurs chased through the partiers.

"I know—" Troy shrugged "—not completely fair, but I can't be accused of driving someone else to pay more since I took the burden of the highest bid upon myself."

Madame Emcee leaned in to the mic. "And it is a quite generous donation, may I add." She nodded to Troy. "But please, continue."

"Since we're all here in support of a worthy cause, I hope my request will be honored by the woman I choose. After all, it would be a double standard if this bachelor auction didn't work both ways."

His cocky logic took root and cheers bounced from person to person like beach balls at a raucous Jimmy Buffett concert. Troy started down the steps with a lazy long-legged lope, microphone in hand. The men and women around Hillary whooped and shouted louder while Troy continued to speak into the mic. He paused at the first row, then moved on to the second and the third, playing the crowd like a fiddle as each woman wondered if she would be chosen. The spotlight followed him farther still, showcasing every angle of a face too handsome to belong to someone who couldn't be trusted to use that charm wisely.

Abruptly, he stopped.

Troy stood at the end of row five. Her row. He stood beside Colonel Salvatore. The older gentleman—her contact—scowled at Troy.

And why not? He was making it difficult for her to stay low profile this weekend, which was what she'd been instructed to do. But then he couldn't possibly know how much trouble he could cause just by bringing the spotlight to this row.

Troy extended his hand and looked Hillary straight in the eyes. "I choose you."

Three

Her stomach fell as quickly as her anger rose, which was mighty darn hard and fast. What game was he playing now? She had no clue.

She did know that every single pair of eyes in this room was glued to her. She looked farther—and crap—her horrified face was plastered right there in full color on the wide screens.

Undaunted, Troy dropped to one knee.

Damn his theatrical soul.

"Hillary—" his voice boomed through the speakers "—think of the children and their scholarships. Be my date for the weekend."

She wanted to shove him on his arrogant ass.

Troy shifted his attention to the colonel. "I assume you won't mind me stealing your date?"

The colonel cleared his throat and said, "She's my niece. I trust you'll treat her well."

Niece? Whatever. Sheesh. This was nuts.

A steadying hand palmed her back. Salvatore. Her skin turned fiery with embarrassment. She turned to him for help.

Salvatore smiled one of those grins that didn't come close to reaching his pale blue eyes. "You should dance, Hillary."

Right. She should get her feet moving and then people would stop staring at her. Determined to feel nothing, she put her hand in Troy's—and still her stomach did a flip. She was not sixteen, for crying out loud. Although his grip felt so warm—callused and tender at the same time. Her body freakin' tingled to life. She'd always prided herself on being in control of her emotions. The second she'd found out what an immoral creep Barry was, she'd felt nothing but repulsion at his touch.

She knew Troy was a liar, a crook and a playboy. Still her body sang at the notion of stepping into his arms and gliding across the dance floor.

Plus, he'd just bid nearly ninety thousand dollars to spend the weekend with her. Gulp.

The pianist began playing. A singer in a red dress cupped the microphone and launched into a sultry rendition of a 1940s love song.

Troy tucked her to his side and led her to the center of the empty dance floor. The spotlight warmed her already-heating cheeks. His silk scarf teased her hand as he held it against his chest and swept her into the glide of the music. She should have known he would be a smooth dancer.

She blurted out, "Is there anything you don't do well?"

"I take it that's not a compliment."

"I don't mean to be rude, but I'm here to work this weekend, not play games."

"Believe me, this is no game." He pulled her close.

She inhaled sharply at the press of his muscled body against hers. He wasn't some soft desk jockey. He was a toned, honed *man*. Her mouth dried and her pulse sped up.

"Just relax and dance." His warm breath caressed her ear. "And I promise not to sing along. Because, in answer to your question, I'm tone-deaf."

"Thanks for sharing. But it's not helping. You can't truly expect me to relax," she hissed, even as her feet synced perfectly with his. His strong legs brushed ever so subtly against hers with each dance step. "You just told a roomful of people and a pack of reporters that you paid nearly ninety-thousand dollars to spend the weekend with me. Me. A woman you've known for less than a day. We've only spoken for an hour."

He guided her around the floor as other couples joined in. The shifting mass of other bodies created a sense of privacy now that all eyes weren't so fiercely focused on them.

"Well, Troy?" she pressed. "What are you hoping to accomplish?"

"Don't you believe in love at first sight?" He nuzzled her hair, inhaling deeply.

She stumbled, bumped into another couple, then righted her steps, if not her racing pulse. "No, I do not. I believe in lust at first sight, but not love. Don't confuse the two."

All the same, she couldn't help but draw in another whiff of his bay rum scent now that she was as close to him as she'd ever been. Swaying, she resisted the urge to press her cheek to his and savor the bristle of late-day stubble. The kind of slightly unshaven look that wasn't scruffy, but shouted *testosterone* to a woman's basic instincts.

But the music slowed and she rested her cheek against his chest, just over the silken scarf for a moment.

"Hmm." His chest rumbled with approval. "So you admit you're attracted to me."

Of course she was. That didn't mean she intended to tell him. "Correction—I was stating that you are simply attracted to me."

He laughed softly, spanning her waist with a bold, broad palm. "Your confidence is compelling."

"Not confidence, exactly." She leaned back to study his eyes. "Why else would you have gone to all this outrageous trouble to spend time with me? Although I guess you're so wealthy that perhaps the obscene amount of money doesn't mean anything to you."

He sketched his knuckles along her jawline. "I wanted the chance to spend time with you."

"Why not go about that the normal way?"

"Tough to do if I'd ended up as someone else's date for the weekend."

"How did you even know I was here?"

"I saw you when I was backstage. My assistant was here. Giving her instructions on what to do was as simple as a text."

"But the ballroom was full of people."

"You could have been in a football stadium, and I would have seen you," he said intensely. His fingers skimmed along the sensitive curve of her neck. "Now let's stop arguing and just enjoy ourselves—unless you plan to renege on the agreement you made in front of all these people. But I have to warn you, everyone will be very disappointed in you if you cost the charity eighty-nine-thousand dollars."

His touch almost distracted her from his manipulative words.

She clasped his wrist and placed his hand back on her shoulder. Her bare shoulder. Maybe not such a good idea after all. "People won't like *you* very much either if you don't follow through on your assistant's bid."

"Everyone knows I've never cared what other people

think of me." His fingers caressed her subtly, enticingly. "But you do care about people's opinions. Rejecting the bid, refusing to play along, causing a scene could all damage your credibility as an event planner—"

"Oh stop it." Stop teasing her. Touching her. Tempting her. "We both know I'm not going to cause a scene, and you're going to pay the charity. How about we shut up and dance in peace?" While she thought about what to do next. At least dancing with Troy gave her an easy excuse to check every face on the dance floor.

He tut-tutted. "My mother always said it isn't nice to tell people to shut up."

"You are really infuriating."

"At least you aren't indifferent."

"That's safe to say." She huffed a hefty exhale. "I want to get this date out of the way so I can go back to my real reason for being here this weekend."

"To check out the chef."

"Right, the food."

Something shifted in his eyes, then his expression cleared again. "Our date is for the whole weekend."

An entire weekend of his touch? His humor and charm? Even with her real reasons for being here, it seemed she didn't have a choice on that. So she could either fight him or use this situation to her advantage.

She could be his "bought for the weekend date," and she could use that role to mingle with everyone, see if she could catch a glimpse of the mystery man Barry had claimed was his business partner. No one would question why she was here and if Colonel Salvatore hadn't liked the idea he would have objected when Troy asked her to dance. Now, people would be too focused on who she was with to worry about why she was here. He would actually make the perfect cover.

All she had to do was resist the overwhelming urge to pull him into a dark corner and kiss him senseless.

Troy had been trying to figure out how to get Hillary away from the crowd for the past two hours.

And yes, he wouldn't mind having her alone after one hundred and twenty-two minutes with her pressed against him, either dancing or tucked by his side as they sampled the array of tiny desserts. The soft feminine feel and minty scent of her was damn near driving him bonkers.

Except he had a plan. He'd already executed the first part through the bidding war. Salvatore's scowl had shot daggers his way all evening, a price worth paying. Hillary could still make her identification, and she would have him as a bodyguard, even if she didn't know it.

He guided her along the pastry line, then over to the drinks table—seltzer water with lime for them both—then out on the balcony where tables were set up. Lights were strung and twinkling, the sounds and smells of the lake carrying on the wind. He picked the table against the wall, overlooking the rest of the small outdoor area and out of clear view of the security cameras.

They could sit beside each other, shielded by the shadows. No one would approach without him seeing them first, and she could watch the party, even though she didn't know they were on the same side. His instincts told him she was honest, but he couldn't risk telling her of his affiliation with Salvatore until both he and Salvatore were certain of her innocence.

Bluesy jazz music drifted through the open French doors. A saxophone player had joined the pianist and singer. All of the musicians tonight were big names who'd donated their talent to the event. One of them was even a buddy from reform school and a Salvatore recruit, as well. This place was crawling with money and agendas.

Including his own.

He took his seat beside her, the handcuffs in his pocket jingling a reminder of his earlier fantasies about cuffing them together—all night long. He tipped back his glass and allowed himself the luxury of studying her out of the corner of his eye. There was no way to hide a woman like her. Sure she wore a simple strapless black gown, her hair clasped back on one side. Yet in a place full of women in designer gowns and priceless heirloom jewels, she stood out from the simplicity of her presence alone. Her unassuming grace, the way she didn't seek the spotlight—and yet, it followed her. She drew the light.

She drew him.

Troy watched her over the top of his glass. "Are you still angry about the auction?"

Slowly, she placed her seltzer water back on the shiny steel table and stirred the lime around deliberately. "I'm upset that you didn't tell me the truth on the airplane. I don't appreciate being lied to."

"I didn't lie." He'd been careful with his words.

She looked up sharply. "You left out parts. You quibbled about your identity." Her freckled nose crinkled ever so slightly in disgust. "Quibbling is the same as lying."

She sounded like Colonel Salvatore. He cursed softly.

"What was that?" She arched a brow, again just like his mentor.

"If I'd told you my full name on the plane, would you have spoken with me during the flight?" He leaned forward, taking her cool hand in his, the minty scent of her carrying on the late-night breeze. "Or if you did speak, would it have been the fun, easy exchange we shared?"

She stayed silent, but she didn't pull away.

"Exactly." He thumbed the inside of her wrist, enjoying the satiny softness of her skin, the speeding throb of her pulse. "I wanted to talk to you, so I didn't pull out a calling card that says hey, I'm the Robin Hood Hacker."

"Okay, okay—" she chewed her bottom lip, which glistened with a simple gloss, all of her makeup minimal "—but can you at least acknowledge that you deliberately misled me?"

"I did." He clasped her hand with both of his and squeezed once. He was making progress. Getting closer. Anticipation thrummed through his veins in time with the bluesy music. "And I'm sorry that has upset you, because honest to God, from the moment I saw you on the plane, I've just wanted to spend time with you. I want you to see *me,* not my Wikipedia page."

She released her bottom lip from between her teeth. "You make a compelling argument."

"Good. Then consider this. We're both here for the weekend. So let's make the most of it. Don't think past Sunday. I'll be patient through all your visits with the chef."

"You don't have to."

"I'm in Chicago because I'm obligated to be here. You've made a dull weekend much more interesting." His eyes lingered on the way the stars and lights brought out streaks of gold in her sleek red hair. His fingers ached to thread through each strand. "If we hang out together for the rest of this gala, we don't have to make awkward conversation with others."

"Better the devil I know than the devil I don't?"

"I can live with that if it means I get to spend more time with you."

Her midnight-blue eyes narrowing, she traced a finger

over the top of their clasped hands. "Are you seriously hitting on me?"

"Yes." And for once he wasn't holding anything back.

"You must be really hard up."

"Or just h—"

"Don't even say it."

"Hungry for your company."

"You're not funny." Her mouth twitched anyway.

"Yes, I am. But it's not something I take pride in. I'm a smart guy, and intelligence is a genetic lottery. What really matters is how I use those winnings."

She swayed forward just a hint. "There's sense in some of that egotistical ranting of yours."

He canted closer until only a sliver of air separated them. He waited. Her breath puffed faster and faster with the quickening rise and fall of her chest. Her pupils widened as she met and held his gaze.

Then her lashes fluttered closed. All the invitation he needed.

Taking advantage of their shadowy corner, Troy slanted his mouth over hers, testing the soft give of her full lips. Tasting the lingering lime flavor of her drink. He squeezed her hand more firmly and claimed her. Completely.

He slid his arm around her shoulder and deepened the kiss, teasing along the seam of her mouth until she opened for him. Her sigh filled him with a surge of triumph. He'd been imagining this since the second he'd clapped eyes on her on the airplane. She didn't just melt, she participated, stroke for stroke.

His fingers tangled in the silky glide of her hair along her shoulders. The strands clung to his fingers with a snap of static and something more snapping through his veins.

There was chemistry here, a connection and crackle he burned to explore along with the curve of her hips, her breasts. He wanted to kiss the crook of her arm, behind her knee and find the places that made her go weak with pleasure. This weekend presented the perfect opportunity to indulge in the countless fantasies exploding to life in his brain.

Her hand flattened to his chest, her fingers gripping his silk scarf and bringing him even closer.

His heart ramped up at the strength of her passion. And the thought of her tugging that scarf off, of peeling the rest of their clothes away and touching him without the barrier of fabric… A possessive growl rumbled deep inside him, almost pushing him over the edge.

He pulled himself from her before he took this too far in such a public setting. She gasped, then looked around quickly.

Her eyes wide, she pressed the back of her trembling wrist to her mouth. "That was…"

"Damned amazing."

"Not a good idea."

"I thought you might say that." But given her reaction to him, he wasn't daunted in the least.

She flattened her palms to the table and drew in a shaky breath. "You've got to understand, I have exceptionally crummy taste in men. It's like I have a radar for finding the most dishonest, untrustworthy guy in the room. So the fact that I like you makes you very dangerous for me."

"You like me." He nudged her loose hairpin back into place. "But, wow, you sure know how to throw a guy hope and smack him back down again at the same time."

"I'm sorry, but it's true, and honestly—" she looked around nervously "—now's also a really horrible time for me to even think about dating."

She seemed to be searching for an escape route, but then he knew that she also needed to stay here, at the party.

Watching. Just as he did. So, pressing her to stay at the table shouldn't be too tough.

He wanted to kiss her again. But he would settle for hearing the sound of her voice, which was more amazing than even the professional singer and musicians back in the ballroom.

"Tell me more about these horrible men you chose."

She started to stand, to leave. "I don't appreciate being made fun of."

He stroked her arm, the heat of their kiss still firing through him. "Stay, please. I'm serious. I want to learn more about you. Unless you have somewhere else to be?"

Pressing two fingers against her temple as if combatting a headache, she looked through the doors at the crowded ballroom, then shook her head. "I should stay until…the chef is free."

"Then pass your time with me. Tell me about the losers."

She turned slowly back to him. "Fine, if you insist." She held up three fingers. "In high school, I dated three guys. One cheated on me." She tucked down a finger. "The other was just using me to get to my best friend." She tucked down another. "Number three liked to mix vodka in his sports drink and dumped me in the middle of the homecoming dance. And the pattern continued on through college and the few times I've risked the whole relationship gig as an adult. I'm some sort of a scumbag magnet."

She said it all dispassionately, as if she'd built a defense against the hurt, but somehow, he knew it was an act. Guilt pinched inside him over the things he wasn't telling her, that he wasn't authorized to tell her. His intermittent work for Interpol depended on him keeping up a carefree, jet-setting lifestyle. But if she ever found out his real reason for being here, she would have to know that for once, someone was actually putting her welfare first.

"Hillary, it's not nice to call me scum."

"I'm sorry, really, but you must be if you're drawn to me. Or maybe it's because I'm drawn to you." Her pupils widened again in response, just as they had right before he'd kissed her.

"Or maybe you're just going through lots of frogs until you find your prince."

Her laughter reached out to him on the night air. "You're mixing up your fairy tales. You're not a prince. You're Robin Hood."

He winced. "God, I hate being called that."

"Robin Hood's been a beloved fella throughout history." She toyed with a lock of her hair. "He took care of the less fortunate. Exposed corruption."

"He wasn't in it for the glory."

Her praise was making him itchy.

"So it's the adoration you object to." She tapped his wrist, already showing a bruise from where he'd first fought the handcuffs earlier. "That's actually rather honorable."

"Watch it. You're falling under my scummy spell."

"Right." She inched her hand away. "Thanks for the reminder."

"I just want to keep you safe from me." He winked.

She rolled her eyes. "I'm twenty-seven. It's time I looked out for myself."

"Does that mean you're going to stop fighting the notion of being my date for the weekend?" This whole weekend would be so much easier if she went with the flow. Easier, yes, but he also couldn't deny he found bantering with her exciting.

Intoxicating.

"I thought the auction was for tonight?"

"No, you didn't." He took her hand again. "But nice try." He kissed the inside of her wrist, lingering.

Her throat moved with a long swallow. She shot to her feet. "About the weekend, I do have to work. I can't spend every waking moment with you."

"I'll just hang out while you work. I can even sample some pâté, give you my opinion on petits fours. My friends say I'm quite enlightened." He slid his arm around her shoulders, pulling her against him so quickly she forgot to protest. "I'm amazingly footloose, too much money and not enough to do. So I'm all yours."

"That's not a good idea." As they moved away from the table and entered the hallway, she glanced over her shoulder, back at the ballroom.

"Why not?" Because if the way they'd danced together was any indication, they could be very, very good together.

She weaved past two women whispering on their way to the restroom, jewel-encrusted clutch purses in hand. "You'll be bored."

He stopped in front of the gilded elevator and jabbed the up button. "Let me make that call. I really can help you, you know." He chose his words carefully, so she would think he meant the chefs, but so she would also realize he could get her more access overall. "If you're with me, you will meet more people, make more connections for your entertaining business."

She looked up at him through narrowed eyes. "Do you think everyone's Machiavellian?"

"I *know* they are," he answered without so much as blinking. "And knowing that makes life easier."

"Troy?" She touched his silk scarf lightly, her blue eyes darkening with...sadness? "That's no way to live your life."

She swayed into him, and he wondered how the hell he'd gotten closer to her at the moment he'd been trying the least. Something about Hillary Wright had him off balance, as it had from the start.

Right now, he wanted nothing more than to head up to his penthouse suite and make love to her all night long. To tell her again and again how damn perfect she was. To show her she could trust he was one hundred percent into her. That he was a man who didn't want to take anything from her. He just wanted to give.

The elevator slid open.

Colonel Salvatore stood alone inside, mirrors capturing his scowling reflection. He held Hillary's little black clutch bag in one big fist. "I've been looking for the two of you."

Four

Hillary's high heels darn near grew roots into the plush carpet as she stared at Colonel Salvatore glowering at her from the elevator.

She couldn't seem to make herself move forward and end this evening with Troy. An amazing evening. Unconventional, sure, but fun. He'd surprised her with an engaging mix of arrogance, humor, intelligence and perception.

Plus, he kissed like molten sin.

She forced her feet to drag forward without pitching on her face. Inside the elevator, she held out her hand for her thrift-store purse. "I must have left it at the auction. Thank you for keeping it safe."

Silently, Troy stepped in after her, and she realized he must be curious about Salvatore even though he'd written off the man as her "uncle" just before he'd whisked her away to dance. She searched for the words to explain without saying things she shouldn't.

"Troy, this is my friend, Colonel—"

"No need, Ms. Wright," Salvatore interrupted. "Troy and I know each other well."

Something dark in his voice, an undercurrent she didn't comprehend, sent shivers down her spine. She looked from one man to the other. Troy slid in the key card to access the penthouse floor and the colonel kept his hands behind his back. She reached to press the button for her floor.

Salvatore shook his head as the doors slid closed. "We're all going together. It's time the three of us had a talk."

Together?

Ding. Ding. Ding. The floors went past.

These two men more than just knew each other. Suddenly she realized that Troy was somehow tied into her reason for being here. Given his sketchy background could he be part of Barry's mess, too? Her stomach plummeted even as the elevator rose.

Although she could swear she'd never seen him with her ex-boyfriend. So many questions and fears churned through her head, stirring up anger and a horrible out-of-control feeling. All her life, she'd tried to play by the rules. She'd worked hard to get ahead and somehow she kept screwing up.

The elevator dinged a final time, opening to a domed hallway with brass sconces and fresh flowers. A door loomed on either side, leading to two penthouses. Troy angled left, guiding them inside the three-room suite that sported a 1920s Great Gatsby opulence.

Any other time she would have enjoyed examining the tapestry upholsteries and dark polished woods—not to mention the breathtaking view from a wall of windows overlooking the Windy City. Skyscrapers and the lake blended together in a mix of modern prosperity with a layer of history. She loved cities, craved the bustle and excitement—the ultimate contrast to how she'd grown up. She rubbed the silver cow charm on her purse and turned to face the two men.

Colonel Salvatore paced with his hands behind his back, his heavy steps making fast tracks over the Persian carpets in the living area. Troy leaned lazily on the bar, flipping a crystal drink stirrer between his fingers.

The silence stretched until Hillary was ready to pull her hair out. "Will someone please tell me what's going on?"

"Fine." Salvatore stopped abruptly. "I expected better from both of you. While you two were playing footsie on the balcony, our guy was slipping away. My sources say he left sometime this evening and is probably already on a private jet out of the country."

Her legs folded and she sank onto the edge of a camel-backed sofa. "*Our* guy?"

Pivoting sharply, Salvatore pinned Troy with a laser glare. "You really didn't tell her *anything* about your role here? Damn it, Donavan, why is it you chose now to follow the rules when you've rarely concerned yourself with keeping me happy in the past?" His sigh hissed between his teeth as he shifted his attention back to Hillary. "Troy Donavan's in Chicago for the same reason you are. To help ID Barry Curtis's associate."

Of course he was.

She'd known the truth on some level, from the moment those elevator doors slid open and Colonel Salvatore said he was looking for both of them. Except, up to the last second, she'd been holding out hope—foolish hope—that she was wrong. Apparently her bad-boy radar was in full working order.

Troy knew about her reason for being here and hadn't said a word to her. He'd made her believe he really wanted to spend time with her. She must have looked so ridiculous to him, talking about needing to see the chef. It had all been a game to him, playing along with her. Likely he'd been keeping this from her even on the airplane.

She forced her attention back to Salvatore's words. For better or worse, she still had to get through this weekend in order to reclaim her life.

"The guy we're after is insanely good at staying away from security cameras. It's as if he has an inside scoop. But I would still like the two of you to review the recordings of tonight's events, make use of Troy's exceptional tech skills and see if you can find even a glimpse."

She struggled to sort through so much information coming at her so fast. "Why do you need both of us to identify him?"

Troy snapped the crystal drink stirrer. "Yes, Colonel, please do enlighten us, because I've been wondering the same thing."

"Some things in life are on a need-to-know basis and neither of you need to know why I chose to play it this way. Troy, my tech guy has forwarded you all the security footage from tonight. I hope to hear good news from you both by morning." He nodded to Hillary. "Your luggage has already been brought here so you can change out of your formal wear."

Share a suite with Troy? She eyed the two doors leading to bedrooms. Where was the colonel staying? "And if we find who we're looking for in the video feed right away, we can all go home? This is over?"

"Troy will contact me in my suite across the hall. Once we've reviewed what you found, you'll be free to leave. If anyone sees you leaving the hotel, let the partiers here think you're spending your weekend together somewhere else."

"You're just sending Hillary back to D.C. unprotected after making her a target?" Troy snorted. "Think again."

A target? Surely, he was exaggerating.

"And don't you think she was every bit as much a target before? Helping us is her best shot at getting back a normal life. Good luck convincing her to do anything your way after the masterfully foolish way you've pissed her off," Colonel Salvatore shot over his shoulder before walking out the door.

The door clicked. Then clicked twice more as Troy secured all of the locks, sealing her inside with him.

Hillary shot to her feet and charged over to the panoramic window, suddenly claustrophobic and needing to embrace the open space of the outside. "I can't believe I was such an idiot."

Troy walked up beside her, hands stuffed in his tuxedo pockets. He didn't look surprised. And why not? He'd been playing her from the start.

"Damn you, Troy Donavon." She smacked her palm on the glass. "I was kicking myself for falling for your act on the plane. I knew better than to trust you, and still I bought into your line of bull only a few hours later. You must have been laughing the whole time at how gullible I was."

"Hey, I'm the good guy. There's nothing wrong with your instincts." Broken stirrer in hand, he tapped the glass right by her hand. "And I can promise I was never laughing at you. I just wanted to keep you safe."

She folded her arms over her chest. "How are you a good guy? I'm working with the colonel to get myself out of trouble because of a stupid choice I made in who I trusted. If the colonel's coercing you to be here as well, that isn't exactly a vote of confidence for the man to keep me safe."

"Let's just say he's a friend and he needed my help—

all of which I'm sure he will confirm." Troy leaned closer, the heat of him reaching out to her in the air-conditioned suite. "When I saw you and realized what you were walking into, I thought you could use some… reinforcements."

"But you lied to me. Again, after the auction." And that hurt, too much for someone she'd just met. "On the dance floor, and every second on the balcony when you didn't tell me you knew why I'm here. When you kissed me. You lied by not explaining you're here for the same reason. You played me for a fool."

His deep green gaze glinted with so much sincerity it hurt. "I wasn't playing you, and I never, never thought you were foolish. My only concern from the second I saw you on the plane has been protecting you from any fallout."

"And seducing me? Is that part of protecting me?" The memory of his kiss steamed through her so tangibly she could swear it might fog the window.

He stepped closer. "Protecting you and being attracted to you don't have to be mutually exclusive."

She pressed a hand to his chest to stop him, that damn silk scarf of his teasing her fingers, making her burn to tug him even nearer. "Doesn't that break some kind of code of ethics?"

"I'm not a cop or detective or military guy or even a James Bond spy." He tossed aside the broken drink stick he'd been holding and pressed his hand over hers. "So, no. Seducing you doesn't interfere with my ethics."

"You're just…what? Please do explain." She stared into his eyes, hoping to find some window into his soul, some way to understand what was real about this whole crazy evening with him.

"I'm a concerned citizen with the power to help out, as you are." His voice rang true, but there was a cadence to his answer that sounded too practiced. There had to be something more to his story, to why he was here. But from the set of his jaw, clearly he didn't intend to tell her.

"Then *why* did you kiss me?" To have that toe-curling moment tainted was just the final slap.

"Because I wanted to. I still do." He didn't lean in, but his fingers curved around hers until their hands were linked. The connection between them crackled all over again, even without the kiss.

God, what was wrong with her?

She snatched her hand away. "Well, that's damn well never going to happen again." She backed away from him and his too-tempting smile. "Would you please set up your computer while I change? We have work to do. I would like to finish as fast as possible so we can say goodbye to each other and to this whole horrible mess."

Hillary locked herself in the spare bedroom and sagged back against the six-paneled door. Crystal knob in hand, she propped herself up. But just barely.

As if the day hadn't promised to be stressful enough, she'd been blindsided by Troy again and again.

She scanned the room, her temporary sanctuary with flock fleur-de-lis wallpaper and a dark mahogany bed. Whereas the sitting area had been wide-open with a wall of windows, this room was heavily curtained, perfect for sleeping or curling up in a French, art deco chaise by the fireplace.

For now, she needed to focus on her suitcase, which rested on an antique luggage rack at the end of the carved four-poster bed. She pitched her clutch bag on the duvet and sifted through what she'd packed for something appropriate to wear. What did a person choose for an evening with a guy she wanted, but needed to hold at arm's length? Confidently casual, with a hint of sparkle for her bruised pride—

Her phone vibrated inside her clutch, sending the purse bouncing along the mattress. She raced to grab the cell—and saw her sister Claudia's phone number.

Claudia had stayed in Vermont with her husband and her three kids, where she taught school and watched out for their mother. Her older sister was the "perfect" person, the strong one who met life on her own terms. She never hid from anything or anyone. She admired her sister and her ability to let go of the past enough to move smoothly into her own future.

Claudia would have never been fooled by someone like Barry.

Hillary thumbed the on button. "Hello, Claudia."

"Is that all you have to say? *Hello, Claudia?*" her sister said with more humor than worry. "Hillary Elizabeth Wright, why haven't you returned all seven of my calls?"

She tucked the phone under her chin and unzipped the side of her evening gown. "I've only been gone a day. There's no need to freak out."

"And what a day you've had, sister," Claudia said, pausing for what sounded like a sip of her ever-present Diet Coke. "You should have told me."

"Told you what?" She shimmied down her dress and kicked it to the side in a pool of black satin.

"That you know Troy Donavan—*the* Troy Donavan, Robin Hood Hacker, billionaire bad boy."

Hillary stopped halfway stepping into her jeans. "What are you talking about? I don't *know* him."

Now who was quibbling with the truth? But she needed to stall and gather her thoughts.

"Then you have a doppelganger, because there are

photos of you with him all over the media. Your Google numbers are through the roof."

Oh great.

Of course they were. She should have known. She yanked her pants on the rest of the way. "I just met him earlier today."

Was it only one day?

"Nuh-uh, sister dear. That story's not flying. He bid a *hundred thousand dollars* for a weekend with you?"

"Eighty-nine-thousand dollars, if you want to be technical." She tugged on a flowy pink poet's shirt. "The reporters must have rounded up."

"*Eighty. Nine. Thousand. Dollars.* Ho-lee crap. I can't get my husband to foot the bill for a waffle cone at the ice-cream shop."

"Billy's a great guy and you've been head over heels for him since you sat beside him in sophomore geometry class."

"I know, and I adore every penny-pinching part of him since he's so generous in other ways." Claudia purred over the phone not too subtly. "I'm just living vicariously through you for a minute. It's nice to fantasize about no mortgage and no diapers. So, spill it. I want deets. Now."

"It's crazy." Hillary fingered her silver chain belt link by link. "I'm sure he's just bored and I said no, which he took as a challenge."

"Then keep right on challenging him until you get some jewelry."

"That's an awful thing to say." She hooked the belt around her waist loosely.

"Ahh," her sister said knowingly. "You like this guy."

"No. I don't. I *can't.*" She flopped back on the four-poster bed, staring up at the intricately carved molding around the tray ceiling. "I haven't known him long enough to draw that kind of conclusion."

"That hot, is he?"

"Hotter."

"You lucky, lucky lady." Claudia paused for a long gulp of her drink. "Did you have a crazy one-night stand with him?"

"God, no." Hillary sat upright. "Since he bought this weekend with me, sleeping with him would feel…cheap."

Still, her mind filled with images of lying back with him on this broad bed until her fingers twisted in the lacy spread.

"I hate to be the one to break it to you, but eighty-nine-thousand dollars isn't cheap, sister."

"You know what I mean."

"I do. I'm just teasing." The phone crackled with the sound of her shuffling the phone from one ear to the other. "Would you have slept with him if there hadn't been the infamous auction?"

"No. Definitely not." She hesitated. "I don't think so."

"Wow." Her sister's teasing tone faded. "He really has gotten to you."

"He's—" a knock sounded on her door "—here. I need to go."

"Call me. Just check in to let me know you're okay." Claudia's voice dripped with big-sister concern. "It's been a tough year for you."

"For all of us." Their father had died of a heart attack in his sleep. Their mother was in rehab—again. And then in her grief, Hillary had lost herself in a relationship with Barry. It was time for luck to swing over to the positive side. "Love you tons, but I gotta run."

She disconnected and reached for the door. Now, she

just had to make it through the whole night without thinking about how Troy's kiss brought her body to life in a way Barry's never had.

Love you tons.

Hillary's voice whispered in Troy's head as he watched her walk deeper into the suite's living room. Who had she been talking to on the phone while she changed clothes?

She'd been buttoned-up sexy in her power suit on the plane. She'd been gorgeously hot in her strapless black gown.

And now she was totally, approachably hot in tight jeans and a long pink poet's shirt with a slim silver chain belt resting low on her hips. She made comfy look damn good.

He pivoted away hard and fast, shoving up the sleeves on his button-down—he'd changed into jeans, too. On the coffee table, he'd fired up his laptop. Now he just needed to log on to the secure network to retrieve the colonel's video feed.

How like the old guy to make sure Hillary was royally pissed off before leaving her here for the rest of the night. Colonel Salvatore had definitely gotten his revenge over the auction stunt.

They'd played back-and-forth games like this since school. Troy would reprogram the class period alarms. The colonel extended evening study period by an hour, which pissed off Troy's classmates, who rained hell down on him in other ways.

Usually the mind games and power plays with Salvatore were fun. But not tonight. At least having Hillary here in his suite made it easier to keep an eye on her.

Troy called to Hillary without looking up from the keyboard, "I ordered coffee and some food in case it turns into a long night."

"I'll take the coffee but pass on the food. Let's not waste time." Her bare feet sounded softly along the Persian rugs. "We have a job to do."

"I've wired my laptop into the wide-screen TV so we don't have to hunch over a computer. The images will be larger, nuances easier to catch." He'd also run the pixilation through a new converter he'd been developing for use with military satellites.

"That looks high-tech, but it makes sense you would have the best toys."

Toys? He wasn't dealing in Little Tikes, but then he wasn't into bragging, either. He didn't need to.

His "toys" spoke for themselves. "You might want to reconsider the food. This will take a while. It's not like watching footage of the night once and we're done. There are different camera angles, inside and outside. We'll be reliving the night five or six times from different bird's-eye views."

"Are *we* on there?" She gripped the back of the chaise.

"We will be. Yes." Would she see how damn much she affected him? Good thing he was in control of what played across that screen.

"What about out on the balcony? The kiss? Is that one on camera for anyone to see?"

"I'm also fairly good at dodging security cameras when I choose." He glanced at her, took in every sleek line of her long legs as she walked to the room-service cart. "I can assure you. That moment was private."

Her footsteps faltered for a heartbeat. "Thank you for that much, at least."

"You're welcome." He grinned and couldn't resist adding, "Although, there's still the film of us dancing so close it's almost like we're—"

"I get the picture. Turn on the TV." She poured a cup

of coffee from the silver carafe, cradled the china in her hands and curled up on a vintage chaise.

He sat on the sofa, in front of his laptop. He split the TV screen into four views. "We can save time using the multiple views on some of the sparser scenes, then go back to single screen for the more populated cuts."

"Why is it that so few people have seen this guy?" She blew into her coffee.

"It's not that so few have seen him. It's that they're all afraid to talk." He fast-forwarded through four squares of empty halls, empty rooms. "You should be afraid, as well."

"Why aren't you?"

"I'm afraid for you. Does that count?"

He slowed the feed of cleaning and waitstaff setting up. Caterers. Florists. Just because their informant said the guy would be at the party didn't mean he couldn't be using a cover of his own. Troy clicked to zoom in on a face with the enhanced pixilation software that could even read the bar code still stuck to the bottom of a box of candles.

Glancing left, he checked for a reaction from Hillary, but nothing showed in her expression except pleasure over the sip of coffee. He took in the bliss in her eyes over a simple taste of java. What he wouldn't give to bring that look to her face. He turned back to the TV mounted over the fireplace.

Even keeping his attention on the screen and computer, he was still hyperaware of Hillary sitting an arm's reach away. Every shift on the chaise, every time she lifted the mug of coffee to her lips, he was in tune to it all.

The air conditioners kicked on silently, swirling the air around, mixing the smell of java with her fresh mint scent. Was it her shampoo or some kind of perfume? He could picture her in a bubbling bath with mint leaves floating around her....

"Troy?"

Her husky voice broke into his thoughts.

He froze the image on the screen. "Do you see something?"

"No, nothing. Keep running the feed." She set aside her china cup and saucer with a clink. "I'm just wondering… How did you meet up with Colonel Salvatore? And please, for once, be honest the first time I ask a question."

She wanted to talk while they watched and worked? He was cool with that. He could share things that were public knowledge. "The colonel was the headmaster at the military boarding school I was sent to as a teenager. He's since retired to…other work."

"You still stay in touch with him?"

"I do." As did a few other select alumni. "Let's just say I'm obligated to him for the life I lead now, and he's calling in a favor."

She slid from the chaise and walked to the room-service cart. She rolled it closer to him and poured *two* cups.

A peace offering?

She set down a cup and saucer beside his computer. "What was your high school like?"

"Imprisoning." He didn't bother telling her about his no-liquids-around-computers rule, especially when the computer was equipped with experimental software worth a disgustingly large amount of money. Instead, he lifted the cup and drained half in one too-hot gulp.

"I meant, what was school like, what was your life like before you were sent to reform school?"

"Boring." He drank the rest of the coffee and set aside the empty china.

"Is that why you broke into the DOD's computer system?" She sat beside him, her drink on her knee. "Because you were bored?"

"That would make me a rather shallow person."

"Are you?"

"What do you think?"

On the screen, the auction area began to fill. He manipulated the focus to capture images of people with their backs to the cameras, reflections in mirrors, glass and even a crystal punch bowl.

She leaned forward, her slim leg alongside his. "I believe you're probably a genius and a regular academic environment may not have been the right place for you."

"My parents sent me to the best private schools—" again and again, to get kicked out over and over "—before I went to the military academy."

"You were bored there, too."

Did she know she'd inclined closer to him?

"Teachers did try," he said, working the keyboard with one hand, draping his other arm over the back of the sofa. "But they had a class full of students to teach. So I was given lots of independent studies."

"Computer work." She set her cup on the far end of the coffee table. "Alone?"

Hell, yes, alone. All damn day long. "The choice was that or be a social outcast in a class with people five or more years older."

She tapped the pause key on his laptop and turned toward him. "Sounds very lonely for a child."

"My social skills weren't the best. I was happier alone."

"How could the teachers and your parents expect your social skills to improve if they isolated you?" Her eyes went deep blue with compassion.

He didn't want her pity. Frustration roiled over how she'd managed to slip past his defenses, to pry things out of him that he usually didn't share. He snapped, "Would you like to tutor me?"

She flinched. "You seemed to have mastered the art of communication just fine."

Anger was his fatal flaw. Always had been. He leveled his breathing. "I have the brotherhood to thank for the social skills."

And the anger management.

"The brotherhood?"

He reached for the keyboard again, setting the screen back into motion, losing himself in the technology of manipulating the image. "Military reform school was a sentence, sure, but I found my first friends there. They were people like me in a lot of ways. I learned how to be part of a pack."

"Military reform school—so they had issues, too?"

"You mean criminal records."

"I'm not judging." She leaned back until her hair slithered along his arm. "Just asking."

Was she flirting? What was her angle? Why was she asking more about him? Regardless, he wouldn't miss out on the chance to reel her in, and perhaps win back her trust.

"A lot of the guys in the school were there because they wanted a military education prior to going into the service." He wrapped a lock around his finger, unseen behind her back. "Some of us were *sent* there to learn to be more self-disciplined."

Touching her hair, just her hair and nothing more, required all the self-control he'd ever gained. But nothing could will away the blood surging south, the hot pounding urge to undress her.

"And you formed a brotherhood with those people, rebels like yourself?"

"I did." That much he could say honestly, and without

mentioning the whole Salvatore/Interpol connection. "Together, we learned how to play within the rules."

She nodded toward the image of him on the runway at the bachelor auction, taking the mic and crowing to the audience about how he'd played them. "You don't look particularly conformist to me."

"You should have seen me back in the day." Hair always too long for regs and an attitude he'd worn like his own personal uniform.

"Do you have pictures of yourself from that time stored somewhere on this computer?" She leaned forward and he let go of her hair quickly.

"Sealed under lock and key. Trust me, you'll never find any old yearbook photos of me."

"Hmm…"

She went silent again, and he wondered what she was thinking. He clicked the computer keys to freeze on the frame of the ballroom filling the screen. She leaned her head on his shoulder.

His body went harder, if that was even possible. He almost reached to pull her over, kiss her again, tuck her underneath him and—

"Troy, there's a photo of me sitting on the Easter Bunny's lap."

What? She was giving him conversational whiplash. "What's so bad about that?"

"I was thirteen."

"Aww…" Now he understood. She'd been trying to make him feel better by sharing her own secret embarrassment. So sweet, he didn't have the heart to tell her he'd left those concerns behind him a long time ago. "Your mom made you."

"Hell, no." She froze the image again and angled sideways to face him full-on. "I was there because I wanted to believe. In the Easter Bunny. In Santa. In the Tooth Fairy. I was teased in school until I learned it was best to keep some things to myself. There wasn't a Sisterhood of the Tooth Fairy at my junior high."

God, she was freaking amazing. After all the ways he'd lied to her, quibbled, maneuvered, whatever, she was still worried about him being hurt by some slights back when he was a kid.

He gathered up a fistful of her hair. "You really are too awesome for your own good."

"Compliments will not get me into your bed," she said, her lips moving so close to his they were almost touching.

His fingers tangled in her hair, he stared into her blue eyes, which were deepening with awareness. "What if I came to *yours*?"

Five

The feel of his hand in her hair, his fingers rubbing firm circles against her scalp, offered a sensual mixture of setting her nerves on fire and melting her all at once. Right now, she wanted to be the type of person who could just lean into him for more than a kiss and damn the consequences. She wanted to do something she'd never done before—have a one-night stand with a virtual stranger. He was so close their breath mingled until she couldn't tell if the coffee scent came from him or from her.

"I told you we were never going to kiss again."

"I heard you. I was there, remember? While I enjoy the hell out of kissing you, it's not mandatory for going to bed together. Admit it," he growled softly, "you're tempted."

"I'm tempted to eat all the marshmallows out of a box of Lucky Charms, but that doesn't mean I intend to do it."

"Never?" he challenged.

"Okay," she conceded. "Maybe I did it once. Doesn't mean that was a smart thing to do."

"Then how about a kiss just for a kiss's sake, so you can prove to me whatever we felt downstairs was a fluke."

A fluke? Oh, she already knew what she'd felt, and it was real. That didn't mean she intended to jump into bed with a guy just because the kiss rocked her socks. Perhaps that was the lesson Mr. Have It All needed to learn. She could turn the tables, knock him off balance with a mind-numbing kiss and show him she could—and would—still walk away. Excitement pooled low in her belly at the thought. She trailed her fingers along his forehead, over the eyebrow with a slash of a scar through it, then cupped his jaw in her hands.

With slow deliberation, she took his bottom lip between her teeth, tugging before teasing her tongue along his mouth. His eyes glinted emerald sparks of desire, and then she didn't see anything. Her eyes closed, she sealed herself to him, her mouth, her chest, her hungry hands and hungrier body.

This kiss was different than the reserved connection on the balcony where there'd been the threat of interruption. Here, they were alone. She was free to explore the breadth of his shoulders, the flexing muscles in his arms as he hauled her close.

Her breasts pressed against the hard wall of his chest. Her nipples tightened to needy buds against him, hot and achy, yearning for the soothing stroke of his tongue. A tingling spread inside her, so intense it almost hurt. She wriggled to get even closer, shifting to sit on his lap, straddling him. And...

Oh. My. She arched into him, against the rigid length of his arousal pressing so perfectly against her.

A purr of pleasure clawed up her throat, echoed by his

growl of approval. Apparently this was a language optional make-out session.

His hands slid from her hair, roved down her back and slid under her bottom. In a fluid move, he flipped her onto her back and stretched over her on the sofa. The weight of him felt good, so very good, intensifying every pulsing sensation. The fabric of the sofa rubbed a sweet abrasion against her tingling nerves.

She hooked a leg over his, throwing back her head as he kissed along her jaw and over to her ear. His hot breath caressed her skin with the promise of how good that mouth would feel all over her body. She tipped her face, shaking her hair back and giving him fuller access as he tugged on her earlobe with his teeth. In an out-of-control moment, she flung out an arm to steady herself. Her fingers clenched the coffee table—

Sending her full china cup clattering to the ground.

Troy froze, then looked to the side sharply before sweeping his computer away from the spilled coffee. The rush of air along her overheated body brought a splash of much-needed reason. What the hell was she doing? She'd only just met the guy and already she'd kissed him twice. She'd wanted to show him how she could kiss and walk away, and she'd ended up beneath him.

Gasping, she swung her feet back to the ground, her toes digging into the plush Persian cotton. The rush back to earth was slower than she expected; her senses were still on tingling alert. Giving in to the temptation to kiss him hadn't been her best idea. She should be focused on the video feed, on finding Mr. Mystery Cohort as soon as—

Squinting, she studied a far corner of the screen, just a hint of a flashy gold ring that looked familiar, with some kind of coin embedded on the top. The fog of passion parted enough for her to process what was right in front of her eyes.

"Troy, hold on a second." She grabbed his shoulder. Her fingers curled instinctively around him for a second before she pulled back.

"What's wrong?" He looked over his shoulder.

"On the TV, can you play with the image for me? There…" She pointed to the top left corner as he righted his computer and sat again. "Can you find a reflection of the face of that guy wearing the ugly gold ring?"

"Of course I can." He dropped back onto the sofa with his laptop, his hair still askew from her frenzied fingers. She seriously needed to rein in her out-of-control emotions.

She clenched her fists against the temptation to finger comb his hair back into place and focused her attention forward. In a flash, the picture zoomed in, with a clarity that boggled her mind. Whatever software he had beat the hell out of anything she'd seen on *Law & Order* reruns. The picture moved and inverted as he shuffled the views, pulling up reflections off a number of sources until…

Bingo.

"That's him," Hillary said, standing and walking closer even though she didn't need any further confirmation. "That's Barry's business partner."

Two hours later, Troy leaned in the open doorway to Hillary's room as she packed her small suitcase.

After she had ID'd the face in the video feed, they'd contacted Salvatore. Troy had only caught one glimpse of Barry Curtis's cohort at a regatta race in Miami, but he agreed the face fit what he remembered. Now Salvatore was off making his calls to contacts. Since they had a face to run through international visual recognition systems, hopefully soon they would have a name. An honest to God lead, a trail to follow. They would have the guy in custody soon.

But in the interim, Troy needed to make sure no backlash came Hillary's way for bringing down a multibillion-dollar international money laundering operation. He needed to keep her in his sights. And lucky for him, thanks to the bachelor auction, going their separate ways wasn't going to be that easy to accomplish. Aside from the fact that everyone in that ballroom had seen them together, the tabloids had snapped photos that were already circulating around the blogosphere. Follow-ups would come their way, questions on how they'd spent their weekend together. She couldn't just duck out of sight, and he couldn't let her stand alone and vulnerable in the spotlight.

He had to admit, time with Hillary would not be a hardship in the least.

Thanks to a pair of killer high heels, her already-amazing legs looked even more train-stopping. Her black tank top and wide belt drew his eyes to every curve he'd felt pressed against him earlier. Curves he was determined to explore at length someday in the not-too-distant future.

He might be completely the wrong man for a rose-colored glasses chick, but that last kiss from Hillary made it impossible for him to turn away. She would be his. The only question was when.

Now that their first goal of the weekend had been accomplished, he would have time with her to figure that out. She might think she was going home to D.C., but he had other plans. He just needed to persuade her.

Hillary flicked her damp ponytail over her shoulder. "What's wrong, Troy? Aren't you happy? We helped them identify the guy." She zipped her roll bag closed. "He won't be able to rip people off anymore. You delivered justice today."

"He's not in custody, and he's smart." Troy shoved away from the door, taking her question as an invitation to enter her bedroom in the shared suite. "If he realizes you're the one who identified him... No, I'm not ready to celebrate yet."

"I'll be fine." Her confidence was hot.

Too bad it was also misguided.

"You're too damn naive about this. You're going to take time off from work and come with me. I know a great, low-profile place where you can put your feet up and relax until this all blows over."

"That he-man act may work with some women, but not with me. I'm going home. The whole reason I came to Chicago was to ID this guy so I could go back to the job I love." She hefted up her suitcase.

He thought about taking the bag from her, but a tug-of-war would likely make her pull back all the more. He sat on the end of the chaise by the window. "You can't return to D.C. Not yet. You need to lie low until the authorities bring him in."

"That's a rather open-ended timeline." She dropped the bag to the ground and sat on it. "I can't just duck out of my life indefinitely."

Good. At least she wasn't walking out the door. "The colonel assures me it will be a week, two weeks tops. Take emergency leave—say you've got a sick mother."

"Sick mom? Really?" She crossed her feet at the ankles. "You think up lies easily."

"Say whatever the hell you want." He tapped the toe of her high heels with his Ferragamo-clad foot. "But let me help."

"No, thanks." She tapped him right back. "I can take my own vacation without you."

His foot worked up to her ankle. "Can you just walk away from this?"

Her lashes fluttered for an instant before she said, "It's just physical reaction."

"Is that such a bad thing?"

"It can be." She pulled her foot back and crossed her legs.

Gorgeous legs. Miles long. The sort made for wrapping around a man's waist.

"Then come away with me for a week, err on the side of caution." He winked. "I promise to come through for you."

"Argh!" She stomped both heels on the carpet. "Can't you just talk to me? Drop the charming, polished act and just speak."

His grin spread. "You think I'm charming?"

She shot to her feet and grabbed her bag by the handle. "Forget it—"

He stepped in front of her. "I'm sorry. I just… I don't want you to leave. What the hell do you want from me?"

"Honesty. Why are you pushing so hard when this is already settled? Our work here is done, and I'm not a defenseless kid."

"Hillary, damn it…" He struggled for the words to convince her when she'd hamstrung him by telling him not to use any charm. Kissing her again wouldn't gain him any traction right now, either. "You confuse the hell out of me. I'm worried about you, and hell, yes, I want to make love to you on the beach in every continent. But I also want time with you."

"Honestly?"

"As truthful as I know how to be. Spend a week with

me. Be safe. Get me out of your system so you can return to your regular life without regrets."

"What makes you think you're in my system?"

"Really? Are you going to look me in the eye and tell me you don't feel the attraction, too? And before you answer, remember I was there when we kissed."

"Okay, I'll admit there's…chemistry."

"Explosive chemistry, but it's clear neither one of us is ready for something long-term. So let's let whatever this is between us play out before we return to our regular lives."

She studied his face, and he could have sworn she swayed toward him. But it was just her head moving back and forth.

"I can't, Troy. I'm sorry." She backed away, pulling her roller bag with her. "I'm going home to Washington, to my normal, wonderfully *boring* life."

Ouch.

There wasn't a comeback for that.

Stunned, he watched her walk away. She was actually leaving, opting for her everyday job in D.C. rather than signing on for the adventure of following their attraction wherever it led. Some might call it ego for him to be so stunned, but honest to God, he was floored by the power of their attraction. He knew it wasn't one-sided. That she would turn her back on the promise of something so unique, so fantastic—so very much *not* boring— blew him away.

He wasn't sure exactly why it was so important to him that he follow her. The attraction. Keeping her safe. The challenge of her saying no. Maybe all three reasons.

Regardless, she'd vastly underestimated him if she thought they were through. If she wouldn't come with him then he would simply have to make do with helping her hide out in the nation's capital.

* * *

She'd actually done it. She'd walked away from Troy Donavan.

That made her either the strongest woman in the world—or the most afraid. Because the thought of spending the next week or two with Troy was the scariest and most tempting offer she'd ever received. Walking away hadn't been easy, and she still didn't know if that made her decision to do so right or wrong.

Her roller bag jammed in the revolving door.

Figured.

She yanked and yanked until finally the door bounced back and released her suitcase. Freed, she stepped outside the hotel, scanning for a cab. She would worry about the expense of changing her ticket return date later.

Of course it was raining, turning an already-muggy early morning all the more humid and dank and overcast. Four more aggressive commuters snagged cabs before her. Exhausted, frustrated and close to tears, she sat on her suitcase again.

"Need a ride?"

Hillary almost fell off the bag.

"Colonel Salvatore?" She steadied herself—darn heels she'd vainly chosen because of Troy. "I'm just trying to catch a cab to the airport."

Her eccentric contact again wore a gray suit and red tie, his buzz-cut hair exposed to the elements. She couldn't help but think about Troy's linen fedora and all the thin-brimmed hats he wore in the photos of him that filled the press.

"Then let me take you. I owe you that, as well as arranging for your change in flight plans."

Resisting would be foolish, and she really did need to leave before she raced back up to Troy's suite—which she couldn't even do since she didn't have a penthouse key card. "Thank you. I gratefully accept."

A driver was already opening the doors to a dark SUV with tinted windows. She slid inside for what had to be the most awkward car ride of her life. Colonel Salvatore didn't speak for their whole drive through the city to Chicago's O'Hare International. He simply typed away on his tablet computer. After five minutes of silence, she focused her attention on final views of the city slicked with rain. Who knew when or if she would return?

Her eyes drifted over to study the colonel, the former headmaster of Troy's military high school. Troy had said he "helped out" but how deeply did that connection go? She'd been working with local authorities when she met the colonel.... None of it mattered. Time to put the past— Barry— behind her and start fresh.

Right?

But once they reached the airport, the SUV didn't stop at the terminal. "Colonel?"

Holding up a hand, he focused on whatever he was working on at the moment.

"Sir," she pressed as the muffled sound of jet engines grew louder, closer, "where are we going?"

He clapped the cover closed on his tablet. "To the private planes. I'm taking a personal jet."

"But I'm going to D.C. Regular coach status is okay with me."

"You have options."

"I've done what you asked me. It's time for me to go home."

"Troy will follow you because he's convinced you need watching until we have everything neatly tied up."

A thrill shot through her before she could steel herself,

an unstoppable excitement over the thought of seeing him again after all. "He's free to go where he chooses."

"Or you could go with him to someplace...different."

Confusion cleared, like the mist rolling away to reveal the line of private jets beyond the colonel's. "He's in one of those planes, isn't he? Is it his personal aircraft or is he waiting inside yours?"

"You're a quick one. Good. Troy needs someone sharp to keep up with him." He nodded toward the row of silver planes nestled in the morning mist. "Mine's next in line, and yes, the one closest is Troy's private aircraft."

"You expect me to just hitch a ride with him? Don't I need to check in or something?"

"I've okayed everything with the pilot. You have your luggage with you." He smiled for the first time. "Admit it. You're tempted to spend time with him. So why not go away with him for a week?"

She bristled at his confidence. "You're awfully sure of yourself."

"Just hedging my bets," he said so matter-of-factly that they could have been discussing breakfast—not the idea of her hopping on a near stranger's plane to go God only knew where.

"You have an answer for everything."

"I study people and make calculated decisions based on how I believe they will react." He straightened his already-impeccable red tie.

"And you're calling me predictable." How could he when she didn't even have a clue what to do next?

"I just bargained on you doing the right thing for Troy."

"The right thing for *Troy?*" That brought her up short. "What are you talking about?"

"I gave you credit for being smarter than this."

She leveled a steady gaze at him and wished she could

wield something a little harsher. She was at the end of her patience here, exhaustion and emotional turmoil having worn her out. "You're not a very nice man."

"But I'm effective."

"Please, get to your point," she snapped. "Or I am leaving."

"I have to agree with Troy that life would be easier and less complicated for all of us if the two of you took a remote vacation. Running around D.C. is too obvious a place for you to be when there is a rich and powerful individual still at large who has reason to be quite unhappy with you and Troy. And if Troy follows you straight to your home, anyone who might be upset over this sting will be able to find Troy, too.... Do I need to keep spelling out all the extremely uncomfortable scenarios for you?"

Her skin went cold. She'd been worried about her future—as in her freedom—but she'd never considered that white-collar criminals might resort to force. "You're not playing fair. And what did you plan to do with me once I ID'd the guy? Did you have a plan to keep me safe?"

"I had hoped we would have the man in custody, and when he got away, I assumed you would be leaving with Troy, based on seeing the two of you together."

The attraction was that obvious to others? "Well, you guessed wrong, and now you're telling me *I'm* responsible for Troy's safety? That's your job, isn't it?"

"I'm doing my job right now. I'm saying what has to be said, for both of your sakes. Get on his plane. By letting him think he's protecting you, you'll be protecting him."

She hesitated.

His eyes flickered with the first signs of something other than calculation or cool disdain. He looked like he actually...cared. "Ms. Wright, please, be the first person in Troy's life to put his interests ahead of your own."

His words sucker punched the air right out of her.

Whether or not his words were genuine or calculated, he'd found a means of coercion so much stronger than force. For whatever reason, she had a connection to Troy, a man she'd only known for a day. He had an influence over her emotions that she couldn't explain.

Maybe it was because she understood what it was like not to have anyone put her first in their lives. Or maybe it was the memory of all he'd told her about his time in school. Or maybe it was that she wanted more kisses.

Whatever the reason, she was climbing on board that airplane.

Dropping his hat on his head, Troy slid from the limo outside his aircraft just as the colonel boarded his Learjet. Ironic. Apparently everyone was getting the hell out of Dodge.

He tugged out his briefcase and jogged through the light rain to the stairs. Once he made it inside, he would need to confer with the pilot about changing their flight plan, rerouting for D.C.

Even with the delay, at least he could work since his plane was a fully outfitted office and completely familiar. He'd built a pod he could move from the hold of any aircraft to another, with an office, a small kitchenette and sleeping quarters. Some seemed surprised at the lack of luxury, but he didn't need the trappings. He had what was important to him: his own portable technological nirvana.

He ducked through the hatch inside and stopped short.

Hillary. Here. On his private jet.

She lounged at his desk, her iPad open in front of her. Early-morning sunrise streamed through a window and outlined her in an amber glow.

Amber glow?

Good God, this woman was turning him into some kind of a poet.

She spun the chair to face him. "I assume that was an open invitation to go with you, but don't gloat. It's not an attractive trait."

He placed his briefcase on the white leather sofa and pulled his hat off. "Well, I certainly wouldn't want to do anything that would make me unappealing to you."

"Good. We're on the same page then." She returned to her iPad and started typing.

"Everything okay?" He resisted the urge to offer her one of the tablets he had on board, prototypes beyond anything the public had seen yet.

"I'm sending a couple of emails to rearrange things at work so I can take an emergency vacation for personal reasons." She looked up. "I'm not comfortable with a convenient 'my mom is sick' lie."

"Fair enough." He placed his hat on his desk in front of her.

She closed her iPad. "Just so we're clear, I'm here for safety's sake. Not for sex."

God, the spark in her eyes made him hot. Although now might not be the best time to point that out.

"Can't be much clearer than that."

"Good. Now where are we going?"

"Monte Carlo."

"Monte Carlo?" she squeaked, her composure slipping. "What about passports?"

"Taken care of. If you recall, when the CIA first questioned you, they required you to turn over your passport to ensure you wouldn't flee the country. Now that you're in the clear, you can have it back. We'll make a brief refueling stop in D.C.—your passport is already there waiting to be picked up." While Hillary talked, he pulled out his phone and typed instructions to his assistant and Salvatore to make sure her passport _would_ be there.

"And what about clothes for me to be gone that long? Appropriate for that locale and weather?"

"Got it covered." He dashed off another text to his assistant before tucking his phone back inside his suit.

"You were that confident I would join you? I'm not sure I like being that predictable."

"Hillary, you are anything but predictable." He scooped up his hat and dropped it on her head, sliding his fingers along the brim.

"Why Monte Carlo?"

"Why not?" He tugged her by the hand to sit on the sofa beside him. He flicked the seat belt toward her and they both buckled in for takeoff.

"Do you live your life that way?" She touched his hat self-consciously. "With a perpetual why not?"

"Works for me." Right now, he was living for the day he saw her wearing that hat and nothing else.

"Why Monte Carlo?" she repeated.

Because he had backup there, and he needed help from someone he could trust. Sometimes, the brotherhood reached out to each other, without Salvatore in the mix. This would be one of those times.

Of all his military school friends, Conrad Hughes, the very first person he'd met on the first day of school, would understand how a woman messed with a man's head. Conrad wouldn't judge. "I'm touching base with a friend who can help cover our tracks. Ever been to Monte Carlo?"

She took off his hat and dropped it on his lap. "I went to Atlantic City once."

"Did you like it?"

"Yes, I did."

"Then you're in for a treat beyond anything the Tooth Fairy would shove under your pillow." He put his hat on, tugged it over his eyes and stretched out to nap.

Six

Monte Carlo was everything she'd imagined—and more.

They'd landed at an oceanside private airstrip near the Ports de Monaco, where a limo awaited them. A thrilling ride later, along the Mediterranean coastline, they'd arrived at a casino that overlooked a rocky cove and packed marina. The beige stucco resort, while clearly pristinely new, had a historical design with Roman columns and arches, statues and sculptures spotlighted in the moonless dark.

Deep inside, there were no windows, but plenty of lights so bright it was impossible to tell day from night. Troy walked through without stopping at the check-in desk. She didn't bother asking questions. She'd already seen how regular rules didn't seem to apply to him.

The air was filled with the cacophony of machines, bells, whistles and gambling calls, but more than that, she heard music, laughter and the splash of a mammoth fountain. Her high heels clicked along the marble mosaic tiles as she and Troy weaved through the crush of vacationers. A mix of languages came at her from all directions, a little like mingling in some of the D.C. parties she'd planned.

Except eyes followed them here. People whispered and pointed, recognizing Troy Donavan.

He pulled off his signature hat. "Let's try our luck once before we head up. Your choice. Cards? Roulette? Slots?"

Exhaustion took a backseat to excitement. Monte Carlo had been in her top ten fantasy places to visit as a kid. She'd researched it, dreaming of James Bond and Grace Kelly. But photos and movies and tabloids just didn't capture the vivid colors, clashing sounds, exotic scents. She'd even fantasized about a fascinating man on her arm, and the reality on that count far surpassed any dreams.

"I'm a little underdressed for cards or roulette." She swept her hands down her jeans.

"You're welcome anywhere I say you are."

Ooooh-kay. "I'm good with a slot machine."

"Fair enough." He guided her to a line of looming machines with high leather bar stools in front.

He offered his hand as she settled in place. Tokens? She'd totally forgotten about getting—

A woman in uniform stopped beside them, smiling at Troy. "*Bonjour,* Mr. Donavan," she said in heavily accented English. She passed him a leather pouch. "Compliments of the house. Mr. Hughes sends his regards."

"*Merci, mademoiselle.*" He opened the pouch and Hillary caught a glimpse of tokens, chips, key cards and cash. He pulled out a fistful of tokens and extended his open palm to Hillary.

"Only one token, thanks. For luck before we go to our rooms to freshen up."

Hillary plucked a single coin from his hand and hitched

up into the chair. *Ching,* she set the lights flashing and waited for the results.... Troy stood behind her, leaning in ever so slightly until his bay rum scent mixed with the perfume of live flowers.

She'd given up trying to understand how she could still be so drawn to, so aware of, a man she knew led a secret life and wouldn't hesitate to stretch the truth if he thought it was "for her own good." Here she was in Monte Carlo and all she could think about was how glad she was to be here with Troy. For the moment, at least, she would embrace the adventure. She would revel in the sensations and refuse to let herself get too attached.

The slot machine ended on a losing note, and she didn't even care. She was here, and her nerves all tingled as if she'd hit a jackpot.

Chemistry. What a crazy thing.

She smiled over her shoulder at him, which brought their mouths so close. She could see the widening of his pupils, see every detail of the scar through his eyebrow. Her breathing grew heavier but she couldn't seem to control the betraying reaction that gave away just how much she wanted his mouth on hers again. She froze, waiting for him to make a move....

He simply smiled and stepped back, offering his hand for her to slide from the high bar stool.

"Whenever you're ready," he said.

Her breath gushed out in a rush. Disappointment over that lost chance for a quick kiss taunted her. She put her hand in his. "Thanks. Or should I say *merci?*"

His hand warmed her the whole way to the elevator, which was made mostly of glass, for riders to watch the whole casino on the way up. Her stomach dropped as the lift rose. She'd always prided herself on being so practical in her plans for her life, but the way she wanted to be with Troy was completely illogical. And now they were as far away from Salvatore, chaperones and intrusions as possible.

What did she want from this time with him while they waited for the all clear from Salvatore?

The answer came to her, as clear as the elevator glass—so smudge-free she almost felt like she could walk right through and into the open air. She wanted to learn more about Troy—and yes, she wanted to sleep with him. She needed to sort through his charm to find out what was real about him, then figure out how to walk away without regrets and restless dreams once she returned home.

The elevator doors slid open as she once again headed to a hotel suite. With Troy.

He palmed her back and guided her into the luxurious, apartment-sized space with a balcony view of the marina. High ceilings and white furniture with powder-blue accents gave the Parisian-style room an airy feel after the heavier Gatsby tapestries of their Chicago penthouse. She stared out at the glistening waters as the bellhop unloaded their bags and slipped away quietly.

Troy walked through her peripheral vision. "Something to drink before we head down for dinner?"

"I didn't sleep at all last night and while you may have had an amazing nap on the plane—" damn his nonchalant soul "—I did not. I just want room service and a good night's rest. Can we 'do' Monte Carlo tomorrow when I'll be awake enough to enjoy it?"

"Absolutely." He tossed his hat on the sleek sofa before walking to the wet bar. "What would you like to drink?"

"Club soda, please," she answered automatically. "Thank you."

He poured the carbonated water into a cut crystal tumbler, clinking two cubes of ice inside. "That's not the first time you've turned down alcohol."

"I told you before." She took the glass from him, fingers brushing with an increasing familiarity. "I don't drink. Ever."

"Have I been around long enough to hear the story yet?" He rattled the ice in his own soda water.

Why not? It wasn't a secret. "My mother was an alcoholic who hit rock bottom so many times she should have had a quarry named after her."

"I'm very sorry."

"It's not your fault."

He brushed her shoulder, skimming back her ponytail. "I'm still sorry you had to go through that."

"I learned a lot about keeping up appearances." She sipped her drink and watched boats come in for the day and others head out with lights already blazing for night travel. "It's served me well in my current profession."

"That's an interesting way of making lemonade out of lemons."

Enough about her and her old wounds. The point of this time in Monte Carlo, for her, was to learn more about him.

She pivoted to face him, leaning against the warm windowpane. "What about you?"

"What do you mean?" he answered evasively.

"Your childhood? Tell me more about it."

"I had two parents supremely interested in appearances—which meant I never had to learn how to play nice. They were always ready to cover up any mistakes we made." His eyes glinted wickedly as he stared at her over his glass.

"Us?"

"My older brother and I."

"You have a brother? I don't recall—"

"Ahh…" He tapped her nose. "So you did read my Wikipedia page."

"Of course I did." She'd been trying to find some leverage, since this man tipped her world about seventeen times a minute. "It doesn't mention your brother."

"Those pages can be tweaked you know. The internet is fluid, rewritable."

She shivered from more than the air conditioner. "You erased your brother from your history?"

"It's for his own safety." He stared into his drink moodily before downing it.

"How so? What does your brother do now?"

"He's in jail." He returned to the bar and reached for a bottle of scotch—Chivas Regal Royal Salute, which she happened to know from event planning sold at about ten thousand dollars a bottle. "If the other inmates know the kind of connections he has, the access to money…"

She watched him pour the amber whiskey into a glass— damn near liquid gold. "What's he in prison for?"

"Drug dealing." He swirled his drink along the insides of the glass, just shy of the top, without spilling a drop.

"Did your parents cover up for him?"

"Periodically, they checked him into rehabs, before they took off for Europe or China or Australia. He checked himself out as soon as they left the continental U.S." He knocked back half an inch.

"You blame them."

"I blame him." He set down his glass beside the open bottle. "He made his own choices the same way I have made mine."

"But drug dealing… Drug addiction." She'd seen the fallout of addiction for the family members, and as much as she wanted to pour that ten-thousand-dollar bottle of booze down the sink, she also wanted to wrap her arms around Troy's waist, rest her head on his shoulder and let him know she understood how confusing and painful his home life must have been.

"Yes, he was an addict. He detoxed in prison." He looked up with conflicted, wounded eyes. "Is it wrong of me to hope he stays there? I'm afraid that if he gets out…"

Her unshed tears burned. She reached for his arm.

He grinned down at her wryly. "You and I probably shouldn't have children together. Our genes could prove problematic. Sure the kids would be brilliant and gorgeous." He stepped back, clearly using humor to put distance between them as a defense against a conversation that was getting too deep, too fast. "But with so much substance abuse—"

"Troy," she interrupted, putting her club soda down slowly. This guy was good at steering conversations, but she was onto his tactics now. "It's not going to work."

"What do you mean?"

"Trying to scare me off by saying startling things."

His eyes narrowed, and he stepped closer predatorily. "Does that mean you want to try and make a baby?"

She cradled his face in her hands, calling his bluff and standing him down, toe to toe. "You're totally outrageous."

"And you're outrageously hot." He rocked his hips against hers. "So let's have lots of very well-protected sex together."

She brushed her thumb over his mouth even though the gesture cost her. Big-time. Her body was on fire. "Abstinence is the best protection of all."

"Killjoy." He nipped the sensitive pad of her thumb before stepping back. "I'll go downstairs and leave you to your rest then. Order anything you want from room service. Everything you'll need is in your room. Enjoy a bubble bath. God knows, I'll be enjoying thinking of you in one."

He scooped up the bottle of Chivas on his way out of the suite.

Great. She'd won. And never had she felt more completely awake in her life.

He sure as hell wasn't going to get any sleep tonight, not with Hillary sleeping nearby.

Without question, he intended to make love to her. But not tonight. He had business to take care of, ensuring he covered their trail and that she was safely tucked away. Then, he would be free to seduce every beautiful inch of her taste by taste, touch by touch, without worry that some criminal would come looking for her.

First, he needed to find Conrad Hughes.

Luckily, the leather pouch included a key card to Conrad's private quarters. At last count, Conrad owned seven, but the one in his casino was his favorite and his primary residence since he'd split with his wife.

The second the elevator doors parted, Conrad was there, waiting. Of course he'd seen Troy coming. Nothing happened in this place without the owner knowing.

"Hello, brother." Conrad waved him inside, brandy snifter in hand. "Welcome to my little slice of heaven."

Conrad Hughes, Mr. Wall Street, and Troy's first friend at the military reform school, led him into the ultimate man cave, full of massive leather furniture and a gigantic television screen hidden behind an oil painting. There was a sense of high-end style like the rest of the place, but without the feminine frills.

Apparently, Conrad had stripped those away when he and his wife separated.

Troy held up the Chivas. "I brought refreshments."

"But you didn't bring your lady friend. I'm disappointed not to meet her."

"She's changing after our trip." Images of her in the spa tub were a helluva lot more intoxicating than anything in the top-shelf bottle he carried. "I figured this would be a good chance to speak with you on my own. Check in, catch up and whatnot."

They had a long history together—two of the three founding members of The Alpha Brotherhood.

Conrad had been a step away from juvie when they'd met in reform school. His crime? Manipulating the stock market, crashing businesses with strategic infusions of cash in competing companies, manipulating the rise and fall of share prices. He would have been hung out to dry by the court and the press, except someone stumbled on the fact that every targeted company had been guilty of using child laborers in sweatshops overseas.

Once the press got hold of that part of his case, he'd been lauded as a white knight. The judge had offered a deal similar to Troy's. Through the colonel's mentorship, they'd learned to channel their passionate beliefs about right and wrong. Now they had the chance to right wrongs within the parameters of the law.

Their friendship had lasted seventeen years. Troy trusted this man without question. And now was one of those times he would have to call upon his help.

His wiry, lanky buddy had turned into someone who looked more like a pro athlete these days than a pencil-pushing businessman. The women had always gone wild over Conrad's broody act—but he'd only ever fallen for one woman.

Conrad had gone darker these days, edging closer to the sarcastic bastard he'd been in the old days. A sarcastic bastard with dark circles under his eyes and a dining tray full of half-eaten food. His friend looked like he'd been to hell and back very recently.

Troy sprawled in a massive leather wingback chair across from Conrad. "I need to tuck Hillary away for a week or so, but I don't want anyone looking for us."

"Is this Salvatore-related or just a need for personal time with a lady friend?"

Conrad was one of the few people on the earth he could be completely honest with. "Started as the first, became both."

"Fine, I can handle things from this end."

Troy trusted Conrad to do what was asked, but he wasn't quite as clear on Conrad's methods, and these days, Troy was more careful about life. Right now more than ever, he couldn't afford to let his impulsive nature take over. Control was paramount.

"Want to share how you intend to do that?"

"Because you're worried I can't handle it? I'm hurt, brother, truly wounded." Conrad drained his drink and poured another.

"Because I want to learn from the master."

"Nice salve to my ego." He smirked. "But I get it. A woman's involved. You can't just leave it all to trust. I can cover for you."

He thumbed on the wide-screen TV and a video of Hillary with Troy at the slot machine played. "I assume this little snippet here was a public display for gossipmongers and the press or you would have used my secure, private entrance."

"Of course it was." He and Conrad had secret access to each other's homes around the world at any time. Yes, he had wanted people to see him with Hillary here, and he should have realized Conrad would have already intuited his plan. "Kudos to your security people for capturing my good side."

"My casino staff aims to please." Conrad cleared the screen. "I'll loop some reels on the security tapes of you, play with the technology so it looks like you're wearing different clothes on different days. My secretary will submit some photos to society pages. The world will think you're here kicking up your heels like a carefree playboy with his next conquest."

"Thanks." He stifled a wince at the word *conquest*. Somehow Hillary had become...more. "I appreciate your help."

"Your plane trip here will cement the story. It would help if you forwarded me some photos from the different airports."

"Consider it done." And that quickly, business was taken care of, which only left the personal stuff. "How are you, brother?"

"I'm good."

"You look like crap. Have you slept recently? Eaten a meal?"

"Who turned you into the veggie police?"

"Fair enough." Troy lifted his drink in a toast. "Just worried about how you're doing since you and Jayne split."

Even the woman's name made Conrad curse.

The breakup had been a surprise to everyone who knew them and so far neither of them was spilling details. Even the social pages had been strangely quiet on the issue and God knows, if either had been cheating, some telephoto lens would have caught something.

Not that his friend would have ever cheated on Jayne. The two had been crazy in love, but a restless traveler didn't work well with a white-picket-fence woman. And those middle of the night calls to assist Colonel Salvatore probably hadn't helped, either.

Conrad rolled his glass between his palms. "Jayne took a job in the States."

"She's a nurse, right?" he asked, more for keeping his friend talking than a need to know.

"Home health care. My altruistic, estranged wife is taking care of a dying old guy, even though she has millions in her checking account. Money she won't touch." His hands pressed tighter on the cut crystal until something had to give. Soon. "She hates me that much. But hey, by all means, don't let my catastrophe of a marriage turn you off of relationships. Not all of them end up slicing and dicing your heart."

He flung his glass into the fireplace, crystal shattering. He reached for the bottle.

"Dude, you really need to lay off the booze. It's making you maudlin."

"And mean. Yeah, I know." He set the bottle down again. "Let's play cards."

"Believe I'll pass tonight. I prefer not to have my ass handed to me." And truthfully, he was itching to get back to Hillary now that he'd taken care of business. But he couldn't leave until he was sure his buddy would be okay.

"You're no fun. And after I did you this great favor."

"Hey, we could play Alpha Realms IV."

"So you can hand me my ass? No, thanks." He thumbed the television back on. "What do you say we catch—"

A sound at the door cut him off short and they both shot to their feet. Hillary stood on the threshold with the leather pouch in her hands and a master access key card in her other hand. "Alpha Realms IV? Really? How old are you two? Ten?"

Conrad set aside the bottle slowly, a calculating gleam in his eyes that had Troy's instincts blaring. *Mine.*

"Ah, so this is Hillary Wright in the flesh. Or should I call you Troy's Achilles's heel?"

Seven

Hillary stood self-consciously in the open archway leading into what could only be described as the man cave to end all man caves.

She'd finished her bath and her meal only to find she'd discovered her second wind. She'd put on a chic yellow silk dress and gone in search of Troy. The guard outside her door had informed her that the leather pouch was her golden ticket to whatever she needed at the casino. Then her own personal body guard had escorted her here to find Troy and his buddy, the casino owner.

Good God, there was a lot of testosterone in this room. Whereas Troy was unconventionally handsome, edgy even, his buddy was traditional: tall, dark, buffed and broody.

Personally, she preferred edgy.

"I'm Conrad Hughes," the dark-haired Adonis extended a not-so-steady hand. "Mr. Alpha Realms's best friend."

Troy hooked an arm around his shoulders. "And he's a perpetual liar, so disregard anything he says."

Like the part about her being his Achilles's heel?

Conrad simply laughed. "As for being ten, yeah. We're men. We're perpetually ten in some aspects."

In which case, she should probably just go. "I'll just leave you to it. I'm sorry I bothered you."

Troy grasped her elbow. "Hold on. I'm done here." He glanced over his shoulder. "Right, bud?"

Nodding once, Conrad said, "We're good. Now go, have fun. What's mine is yours. Nice to meet you, Hillary."

She was back in the elevator with her guard excused before she could register being ushered out. "I think you and your buddy Conrad both need to sleep it off rather than play video games."

"I'm not drunk. Not even drinking anymore beyond the one I had in the room and one when I came down here." He brushed his lips across her forehead. "You're welcome to check my breath."

She tipped her head to his, their mouths so close. And as she looked deeply in his eyes, she could see he was completely sober. He hadn't lied. He'd controlled himself. There hadn't been some "out with the boys" bender. He was here for her, and that was definitely more intoxicating than alcohol.

"I'm not sure I understand you."

"Hillary, the last thing I would do is show up drunk in our room. You have understandable issues on the subject. If I stumbled in sloshed I would be less likely to score."

And that fast he eased the tension that had been growing too heavy and fast for her.

Laughing, she strode ahead of him out of the elevator, back at their suite. "Oh my God, did you really just say that?"

She glanced over her shoulder and caught him watching her with unmistakable appreciation.

"I did. And you're a little turned on." Walking behind her, he stroked a finger up her spine. "Admit it."

Hell, yes. She was burning up inside from a simple touch along her back.

"I'm a little exasperated." She bantered right back without brushing his hand away. Funny, how she was becoming more and more comfortable with his hands on her. Maybe too much so.

"Let's see what I can do about that."

She spun around, hand on her hips. "Seriously, are you suffering from some kind of Peter Pan syndrome? You crack jokes at inappropriate times and you still play video games."

"I develop software, yes."

Her thoughts screeched to a halt. She was learning fast to pick apart his words since he had a deft way of dodging questions with wordplay. "Not just video games?"

"Did I say that?"

There was something here. "Why do I get the sense you're toying with me?"

"Maybe because I would like to toy with you, all night long." His hands fell to rest on her shoulders. "But we need to leave Monte Carlo first thing in the morning so you really should get some sleep."

"We just got here. I thought we were going to play." Is that what she wanted? To play? All she knew was that she didn't want to say goodbye to him, not yet.

"We didn't come here to play. We came here to get you out of the public eye." All lightheartedness left his gaze and she saw the cool calculation at the foundation of everything he'd done. "First thing in the morning, we're going to leave through Conrad's private entrance. The world will think we're here in Monte Carlo somewhere, in case anyone's looking."

"Where are we really going?"

"To my house."

His house? She struggled to thread through his rapidly changing plans. "Didn't you say you live in Virginia? Doesn't that defeat the whole purpose of lying low?"

"I said I'm from Virginia. I do have my business based there, the corporate offices. But I have a second home where I get away to do the creative part of my job—or just to get the hell away, period."

With each word he confirmed there was so much more to him than she'd realized. She hadn't looked below the surface, not really. Maybe because the steady logical man in front of her made the charming playboy all the more appealing. "Where would that be? Who knows where we're going? I'm all for hiding out, but there needs to be someone to look for us if we fall off the planet."

"Smart woman. I respect that about you." He cradled her face in his hands, thumbs grazing her jaw, the calluses rasping over her tingling skin. "I assume you trust Colonel Salvatore."

"As much as I trust anyone these days. The whole trust thing is…scary."

"Good. Those concerns are there to keep you safe in life." With a nod, he stepped away. "We'll make a pit stop at Interpol headquarters in Lyon, France, and update him personally on our way."

"On our way to where?" Her eyes followed him as he walked toward his room without pressing her to accompany him. Which of course only made her want to go with him all the more.

"Costa Rica. But before we get there, I have a surprise."

* * *

Dinner in France?

Hillary was blown away by Troy's incredibly thoughtful surprise. He'd remembered her wish to talk to the chefs in Chicago, and he'd taken that dream up a notch.

Some of the finest chefs in the world worked in Lyon. She'd expected to zip into Interpol and be whisked right out of the country. But Troy had given her a hat of her own and sunglasses, changed his signature fedora for a ball cap and they'd become typical tourists in a heartbeat. After an early dinner, he'd suggested a sunset walk at the municipal gardens—*Jardin botanique de Lyon*—in the Golden Head Park. *Garden* didn't come close to describing the magnificence of everything from tropical flowers to peonies and lilies, to a massive greenhouse with camellias over a hundred years old.

The scent alone was positively orgasmic.

His hand wrapped around hers felt mighty damn special, too.

Holding hands while walking in the park was something so fundamental, so basic anywhere in the world, yet she strolled with a world-renowned guy in France, no less. Still, he made it seem like an everyday sort of date.

And there was no question but that this was an honest-to-goodness date.

Of course, this was the guy who'd cut his teeth on breaking into the Department of Defense's network. Who was he, this man who ran in such high-profile circles but appreciated simple things? A man who worried so deeply about his brother, even as he pretended to cut himself off from deeper feelings with a carefree attitude?

Troy was getting to her, in spite of all her wary instincts shouting out for self-preservation. She wanted for once to find out the yearnings of her heart could be trusted.

She leaned in to smell a camellia. "Why did you do it?"

"Do what?" His thumb caressed the inside of her wrist.

"Really?" She glanced sideways at him through her lashes. "Doesn't everyone ask you about it?"

He brushed an intimate kiss along her ear. "Why did I break into the Department of Defense's computer system?"

"Yeah."

"I told you already." His mouth flirted closer to the corner of her lips. "I was bored."

"I'm not buying it." She spoke against his mouth.

"Then you tell me. Why do you think I did it?" Pulling back, he held her eyes as firmly as he held her hand.

She studied him for a second before answering honestly. "I think you want me to say something awful so you can get pissed off."

"Why the hell would I do that?" He scowled.

"And yet, you're getting pissed anyway, which gives you a convenient wall between us." She tapped the furrows in his forehead.

He backed her against a roped-off area. "You want more? Walls down, total openness and everything that comes with that?"

"You'll only find out if you answer." She smoothed aside the long hair on his forehead, his normally cool-guy 'do pushed down by his ball cap. "If you don't want to tell me the real reason, just say so, but it's unrealistic to think people—especially people close to you—wouldn't want to know."

"You're close to me?" He linked both arms around her, bringing her closer.

"Aren't I?" Butterflies filled her stomach as she thought about how close she wanted to get, how deeply she wanted to trust Troy.

His arms fell away and he backed away a step. "Okay,

fine..." He whipped off the cap and thrust his hands through his hair before jamming the hat on his head again. "Everyone says I had this altruistic reason for what I did, but honest to God, I was unsupervised, spoiled and pissed off at my parents for not—hell, I don't know."

"You did it to get their attention." An image of him as a boy started to take shape, one that tugged at her heart. She suspected there was more to the story but that he was only going to tell her at his own pace.

"I wasn't five." He steered her out of the way of an older couple snapping photos of flowers, touching her with such ease, as if they were lovers. "I was fifteen."

"But you weren't an adult."

"Lucky for me or I'd have been in prison." He stuffed his hands in his suit pockets. "Hell, if I'd done the same thing today, even as a teen, I wouldn't have gotten off so easy."

"So the brotherhood, the guys like you at the military high school, they were really more of the family you never had."

Defensiveness eased from his shoulders. "They were."

"The casino owner? He's a brother?"

"What do you think?"

Her mind skipped to the obvious question. "What did he do?"

He hesitated for an instant before shrugging those broad shoulders that endlessly drew her eyes. "It's public knowledge anyway. Remember the big fluctuation in the stock market a little over seventeen years ago?"

"No kidding?" She gasped. She'd only been about ten at the time, but her teachers had used it in a lesson plan on government and economics. Newscasters and economists still referred to it on occasion. "That was him?"

She sank down on a park bench as other tourists milled past.

"He accessed his father's account, invested money, made a crapton. So his dad let him keep right on investing." He sat beside her, his warm thigh pressing against hers. "But when he caught a couple of his dad's friends assaulting his sister…"

"He crashed the friend's business?"

Troy stretched his arm along the bench, touching her, taking part in more universal dating rituals. "He did. And once he was in the system, he uncovered a cesspool of companies using child laborers overseas. The press lauded him as a hero, but he never considered himself one since his initial intent was revenge."

"So even though what he did was wrong, he had an emotionally intense reason for it, as did you."

"Don't try to glorify what we did. Any of us. We all broke the law. We were all criminals heading down a dark path that would have only gotten darker if we hadn't gotten caught." He tugged a lock of her hair, bringing it close to his face and inhaling. "There was this one guy—a musical prodigy—whose parents sent him to reform school instead of to drug rehab."

She turned on the bench, sliding her hand under his suit jacket to press against his heart. "That had to be painful for you to see, because of your brother."

He didn't answer, just stared back at her with those jewel-tone green eyes, and she wondered if he would kiss her just to end the conversation. She wouldn't stop him.

Then something niggled in the back of her brain. "I think what you did had something to do with your brother."

He looked down and away.

"Troy?" She cupped his face and urged him to look at her again. "Troy?"

"My brother failed out of college, enlisted in the army, then got busted and sent to jail." He held up a hand. "I'm not defending Devon. What he did was wrong. But there were others in his unit dealing, and two of them got off because their dads were generals."

Her heart broke over the image of a younger brother dispensing justice for his older brother.

"Once I got into the system, I stumbled on other... problems...and I decided I might as well do a thorough job while I was in there."

"Wow..." She sagged back. "You sure set the world on its ear."

"The irony of it all? My dad used his influence to keep me from serving time." He bolted to his feet. "Time's up. We need to head back to the airport."

He didn't take her hand this time. Just clasped her elbow and guided her back out of the gardens. His expression said it all.

Date over. There would be no kiss at the door. And honestly, as vulnerable as she felt right now, she could use a little emotional distance herself.

On a plane leaving Lyon, France, Troy knew he should be pleased with how his meeting had gone today with Salvatore at Interpol Headquarters. His plans were falling into place. Hillary was safe. The world believed they were sharing a romantic week in Monte Carlo. No one except the colonel and Conrad knew about their true destination as they flew through the night sky.

Costa Rica.

They would be there by sunrise. He should be pleased, but still he felt restless. Unsettled.

Hillary was snoozing in the sleeping compartment. The transferable pod made his location less traceable as he came and left in different crafts, while still having all of his personal comforts available.

He preferred his life simple, although he couldn't miss the excitement in Hillary's eyes over dining in France. She'd told him from the start that she'd chosen her job to get away from her rural roots, that she was looking for glamour and big-city excitement. He could give her that, and he wanted to. Although he could do without more soul-searching, like what they'd done in the gardens. But he also wondered how she would feel about his more scaled back lifestyle in Costa Rica. He knew his life was not what anyone would call simple, but amidst the travel and business, he preferred things to be…less pretentious, less complicated.

Maybe those days in the military school had left an imprint on him in ways he hadn't thought about before. At the academy, all he'd had was a bunk, a locker trunk and his friends. He'd lived that way even after leaving school and growing his hair again, even with clothes as far from a military school uniform as he could make them. He'd kept his world Spartan, when it came to letting new people into his life. Until now.

Right now, he felt like that fifteen-year-old kid whose life had been turned upside down, leaving him on shaky ground as he figured out who to trust.

Troy tossed his uniform hat on the bottom bunk along with his day planner, pissed off, as usual, and he was only six months into his sentence. "What the hell are you doing here?" he asked Conrad, who was pretending to be asleep.

Conrad called from the top bed. "You're blowing my cover."

"What cover?"

"That I missed formation because I fell asleep," he said,

his voice echoing in the barracks, which were empty other than one other guy who actually was snoozing. "What's your excuse for blowing off a mandatory formation?"

"I got my ass handed to me in trig class today. Just didn't have the stomach to get ripped again by Salvatore because of imaginary spots on my brass buckle."

Conrad extended an arm with his spiral notebook, marked Trigonometry. "Be my guest. Can't help you with the buckle, though."

"Thanks."

Conrad dropped the book and Troy caught it in midair, accepting it without hesitation. He'd helped Conrad out last week with hacking into a news site for stock returns. The limited computer access hadn't been quite as tight as they'd claimed. Except in one realm. "How is it that I can get into any system except where they keep their tests?"

"Uh, hello, they know you're here." His arm arced down and he swatted Troy with a pillow. "They must be paying Bill Gates a fortune to keep that out of reach."

"Funny." Not. It was frustrating being confined to this place. He flopped back and started thumbing through Conrad's notes. Notes that were damn near Greek. "Must be nice being a friggin' math genius."

"If I was a genius I wouldn't have gotten caught. I would be at some after-homecoming dance getting blown by a debutante who gets off on the fact that my old man is rich enough to buy me a Porsche for my sixteenth birthday."

"I think you wanted to get found out."

Conrad ducked his head to the side, looking down. "You think I wanted this? You're nuts. Why did you do it?"

"I'm not sure. 'Mommy' and 'Daddy's' attention instead of a new toy? Fame and recognition? Who knows? The court-appointed shrink just says I'm antisocial." And

how damn weird was it that now, here, he finally had a real friend. "How did you get caught?"

"I let a female knock me off my game. I got sloppy. It's my own fault. Women have always been my weakness. Take it from me, man. Never let a woman be your Achilles's heel." He ducked back to rest on his own bed again. "But you, you never do anything you don't mean to."

In his six months here, he'd never seen Conrad's confidence shaken.

"Sure, I do, Hughes. I blurt out crap all the time that I don't mean to say. Teachers really hate that, by the way."

His buddy laughed, shaking off some of the darkness. "So I see every day. You do take the attention off the rest of us, and for that, we thank you, man."

From the far corner, the guy he'd thought was asleep jackknifed up and threw two fistfuls of brass buckles across the room. "Do you think you two could hold it down? Take the belt buckles, just go and let me sleep in peace. I've got some sort of stomach bug. Leave or you might catch it."

Stomach bug? The loser was probably coming down off something. He was some piano prodigy who'd been busted for drugs and shipped here.

Troy tossed a belt buckle. "No, thanks, Mozart. I'll pass on Marching 101."

"Really, dude—" Mozart swung his legs over the side of his bed, holding his stomach and wincing "—if you would stop worrying about being a moody whiner all the time, you could learn something. To infiltrate the system, learn to work it from the inside. Use those brains of yours to play the game. Polish your damn brass."

Conrad did that uppity sneer thing he had down to an art form. "You're actually telling us to kiss ass, Beethoven? Because you sure as hell don't."

"*Exactly.*" Mozart/Beethoven grabbed the Pepto-Bismol from his bedside table. "*There are other ways....*"

Troy scooped up a remaining buckle and tossed it from hand to hand. "*You make people laugh. Good for you. That's your gig. You're a people person.*"

After guzzling a quarter of the bottle of stomach meds, he swiped his wrist over his mouth, smearing away the pink stain. "*Studies say that a sense of humor is the true measure of intelligence.*"

"*Just because you took that psychology class, Bach, don't think you can trick me into doing things your way by playing mind games.*"

"*Whatever. I'm offering you a new tool for your arsenal.*" Mozart/Beethoven/Bach—aka Malcolm Douglas—shrugged, stretching back out again. "*It's up to you if you want to take it.*"

"*Knock-knock jokes, Douglas?*" Troy tossed the final buckle back. "*Are you for real?*"

Douglas applauded. "*See, that was well-played sarcasm. You've got potential.*"

The door exploded open across the room.

Colonel John Salvatore stood framed in the opening. "*Gentlemen, you'd damn well better be hurling right this second or you will be by the time I'm done running you.*"

Troy shoved up from his computer workstation and pushed open the door to where Hillary slept. Curled up on her side, she hugged the wool blanket he'd picked up on an African safari. Her red hair splashed an auburn swath over the white Egyptian cotton. His hand itched to cup the curve of her hip. He ached to slip into bed and lie behind her, tucking her body into his. He would wrap his arm around her waist, the undersides of her breasts resting against his skin. He would breathe in the scent of her shampoo, stay right there until she woke up and rolled into his embrace, inviting him to indulge in more.

Indulge in everything.

He wanted Hillary in his bed for real, not just to sleep, and he had wanted that since he'd first seen her. But he needed to have his thoughts in order, be in control of himself. He wasn't the impulsive teen anymore who blasted through security firewalls without thinking of the consequences.

And as he thought this through, he was beginning to realize his preference for keeping things simple wasn't going to work with her. She was the type of woman that asked for, demanded, more from a man. She had a way of getting him to talk that no one had managed before. Maybe because she wasn't some groupie who glamorized what he'd done. Even when she didn't agree with his choices, she listened. She wanted the real story.

That was mighty damn rare and enticing.

As he watched the even rise and fall of her chest as they powered across the ocean toward the Costa Rica coastline, he couldn't deny it any longer. He would do anything to sleep with her. Anything.

And he would need everything he'd learned from Salvatore, from Hughes and from Douglas to win her over.

Eight

His Costa Rican getaway wasn't at all what she'd expected.

She slid out of the Land Rover, sounds of the tropical wilds wrapping around her. The chorus of isolation, of escape, echoed. Birds and monkeys called from the dense walls of trees. His home rested on a bluff, with a waterfall off to the side that fed into a lagoon. Wherever he looked out from his home, he would have an incredible view.

Sure, it was a pricey pad, without question. But not in a flashy way. She'd expected a sleek beach place with gothic columns and swaths of gauzy cabanas on a crystal-white beach.

Instead, she found more of a tree house. The rustic wooden structure was built on stilts—which made sense for surviving fierce storms. Built in an octagonal shape, its windows provided a panoramic view of not only the water but also the lush jungle. Splashes of blooming colors and ripening fruits dotted the landscape like tropical Christmas lights.

This wasn't a beach vacation place for parties. This was a retreat, a haven for solitude. There wasn't even a crew of servants waiting. She carried a travel bag while Troy unloaded their luggage. He'd been strangely pensive since their flight, studying her like a puzzle to figure out.

Although she was probably looking at him in exactly the same way.

He glanced over. "Elevator or stairs?"

"Stairs," she said without pause, "I wouldn't miss a second of seeing this from all angles."

Climbing the winding wooden stairs, she drew in the exotic perfume of lush fertility seasoned with salty sea air. The spray of the waterfall misted the already-humid morning air. She cleared the final step to the wraparound balcony.

The man who would choose this type of home intrigued her, and she suspected the house would only get better. She wanted to believe that, as if the house was an indicator of the real Troy. It was ironic that after she'd fought so hard to leave the isolation of the farm, that somehow this secluded place felt amazingly right.

He ran his fingers along a wood shingle, and it opened to reveal an elaborate panel of buttons and lights. He'd keyed codes into elaborate security gates along the drive to the house. Apparently there was a final barrier to breach. He pressed his palm to a panel and the front door opened.

She stepped into a wide space full of rattan sofas and chaise lounges with upholstered cushions of deep rusts and greens. With the windows, it seemed as if the inside and outside melded seamlessly. No period pieces or antiques.

Just well-constructed comfort.

Troy tapped another small panel on the inside wall and

the lights came on. "There are multiple bedrooms. You can choose which suits you best. We're on our own here, so no worries about where the staff might sleep."

Music hummed softly; ceiling fans swirled. "Is the whole place wired like a clap on/clap off commercial?"

"A bit more high-tech than that, but yes. I may dress better these days—" he sailed his hat toward a coat tree with perfect aim "—but I'm still the same computer geek inside. The whole place is wired for internet, satellite, solar panels."

"Everything here is fresh. I thought there wasn't a staff?" The place had clearly been serviced, from the fresh basket of fruit on the kitchen island to the thriving plants climbing toward the vaulted ceiling.

"There isn't an official crew here. Not full-time, anyway." He set their luggage by a sofa. "A service comes in once a month to air the place out, dust the knickknacks. Fill the pantry before I arrive. Then they leave. I come here for solitude."

"But you brought me."

"Yes, I did," he said from beside the fireplace, one foot braced on the stone hearth. "That should tell you how important you are to me."

The seriousness of his statement caught her off guard. "Does that line usually work with women?"

"Your choice. Trust me or don't."

And that's what it all boiled down to for her. Trust. The toughest of all things for her to give. "Could I just give you my right arm instead?"

He shoved away from the wall. "What do you say we take this a step at a time?"

With each step that brought him closer, her temperature rose, her desire for him flamed even as wariness lingered. "What do you mean?"

"Rather than jumping all-in, you can test the waters, so to speak." He lifted a strand of her hair, sliding it between his fingers with slow deliberation.

"Test the waters how?" Like make out on the sofa? Play strip poker? Progress to third base? Nerves were stirring her into a near hysteria, because if her body ignited when he was just touching her hair, there wasn't a chance in hell she would be able to hold out against a full-out touch. And there was nothing and no one here to stop them.

He let her hair go shimmering free. "Go swimming, of course. So which will it be? The pool or the waterfall?"

Hillary stripped out of her travel clothes, a dress she'd slept in on the plane. She needed a shower, but since they were heading to the waterfall... She would just take shampoo with her.

Her suitcases waited at the foot of the bed, but the open doors on the teak wardrobe showed rows and shelves full of clothes, all her size.

He truly had prepared for her visit. What would he have instructed buyers to choose for her? She thumbed through sundresses, jeans, shorts, gauzy shirts—and a half-dozen swimsuits with sarongs. Two-pieces and one-pieces, giving her choices.

One-piece, for sure. She tugged out a basic black suit and stepped into it before reaching for the phone to check in with her sister. Her hand half in and half out of her bag, she paused. What did a call from Costa Rica cost? And would it be traceable, thus risking their safety? She should probably check with Troy on that.

She yanked on a matching cover-up, then stuck her head out the door. "Troy?" she called out. "What're the rules on phoning home? I meant to call my sister while we were in France, and I, uh, forgot."

Their date had so filled her mind, she'd lost sight of everything else.

"Use the phone by the bed," he answered from somewhere around the kitchen. "It's a secure line."

"Thanks, I'll only be a minute."

"Take as long as you need." The sound of cabinets opening and closing echoed. "The only rules here are that there are no rules, no schedules."

She slid back into the room, the easy exchange so enticingly normal, so couple-ish. Plus a ka-billion-dollar vacation home and a world-renowned computer mogul she'd met while they both helped international law enforcement solve a case.

Yeah, totally normal.

And how would she even know "normal" if it bit her on the nose? She certainly hadn't seen a lot of healthy relationships in her life.

Sagging onto the edge of the bamboo-frame bed, she dialed her sister's number from memory. Since there was only an hour's time difference, her sister should be awake. The ringing connection was so clear, she could have been calling from next door. Of course Troy had crazy good technology.

"Uh, hello?" her sister said hesitantly, probably because the caller ID wouldn't have been familiar.

"It's me, Claudia, not a telemarketer."

"God, Hillary, it's great to hear your voice. How's Monte Carlo? Are you winning a fortune? The photos of you are gorgeous, by the way." The sound of Claudia sipping her signature soda filled the airwaves for a second. "I've been saving everything I can get my hands on and downloading the computer articles so you can see it all when you get home. We could have a scrapbooking weekend to organize everything."

Monte Carlo. Their cover story. Telling her sister everything would only worry her so she simply said, "Thank you. You can show me when I visit next."

"We could both be in our retirement rockers by then. Try to make it sooner."

"Fair enough. I promise." She always promised, but when push came to shove, somehow something always interfered.... And why? Her sister was wonderful; her brother-in-law was a great guy. She loved the kids. Their family was actually an example of how a healthy family *could* work. Had she avoided them because it was painful to see everything she didn't have? "I just wanted to check in and tell you I love you. I'll send the kids cool T-shirts."

"How about just have fun with that überhot guy. He beats the hell out of Barry the Bastard Cutthroat."

"He does. He really does. I'm actually getting some of that R & R you're always telling me I need. We're going swimming in a few minutes."

"Please tell me you're wearing a sexy two-piece so I can continue to live vicariously through you."

She looked down at the conservative black swimsuit with the simple black cover-up. "Um, sure."

"Atta girl. You deserve to play, date, flirt. Everything doesn't have to be intense. Enjoy the chase. Love you, but I have to run to clean the guest room."

"You're having company?"

"Uh...yeah. Listen, I really need to go. The kids are killing each other over who gets the last packet of gummies. Bye—" The phone connection cut off.

Phone still pressed to her ear, Hillary eyed the open wardrobe and that stack of bathing suits.... She tossed the receiver down and bolted across the room. Before she could change her mind, she tore off the black suit and snatched up an aqua-colored bikini, crocheted with flesh colored lining. It was suggestive and sexy and something she never would have dared pick out for herself.

If it had been the only suit on the shelf, she might have been angry. But there was such a wide range to choose from, this wasn't forced on her. The store tags on everything made it clear the items had been bought for her.

And she felt good wearing it.

She pulled on the frothy cover-up that matched, the nearly sheer silk sliding seductively over her skin like a lover's kiss. She arched up on her toes to snag a beach towel from the next shelf up. The white-and-black patterned cotton slid down in a tumble all around her, a huge towel made for sunbathing. She whipped it forward to refold…

What in the world?

Blinking, she looked again and sure enough, Troy had somehow, someway ordered a towel with a big Holstein cow pattern. No way could this be coincidental. The man was too smart and too observant. He had to have noticed her cow-patterned luggage tag and the silver pin on her evening bag.

Her sister was right. Things didn't have to be intense. She could play. Flirt. This wasn't an all-or-nothing proposition. A guy who gave cow towels definitely understood the lighter side of life. Her bruised heart could use some soothing after all she'd been through the past month.

Cow towel cradled to her stomach, she charged through the door, ready to meet her adventure head-on.

Troy needed to give his assistant a big fat bonus.

Palm flat against the kitchen counter, he took his time staring at Hillary from head to toe. There were no words other than *wow*—just wow—for how mouthwateringly hot she looked. The sea-green, almost-sheer cover-up rippled over her skin like waves of water, touching her in all the places he ached to caress.

He'd told his assistant to order a variety of clothes for any occasion. His only specific instruction had been to include a few cow-patterned accessories for fun. His assistant had been smart enough not to question or laugh.

That's why he paid her well.

He cleared his throat. "Did you find everything you need?"

"And more." She held up the cow-patterned towel. "This is amazing. Thank you."

"Thank my assistant. She did all the work."

"I'm guessing that she didn't decide on her own to pick out a beach towel with a bovine theme."

"I may have given her some direction. I'm glad you like it." He couldn't wait to see what she thought of the other surprises he'd ordered for her.

His own personal mermaid walked toward him, stealing a little bit of his sanity and will with every long-legged stride. Her eyes slid over him, lingering on his black board shorts and plain white T-shirt with the sleeves cut off.

She held up a small beach tote. "Do you mind if I wash my hair at the waterfall?"

He slid an arm around her and pulled her flush against him. "You can do any damn thing you want to."

"I do believe that's a compliment." She shook her hair back to glide down her spine.

"All that and more." He placed a floppy sun hat on her head before reaching for his straw fedora.

Hooking an arm around her shoulders, he grabbed his own bag of supplies for their morning—food and more towels. He guided her through his house and out onto the balcony. Her jaw dropped in awe, her feet slowing as she looked around her. For a moment, he saw his house through fresh eyes. Somewhere along the line, he'd lost sight of the details, just seeing the place as home.

The space widened into a veranda with a hot tub and a sunken pool built up to the edge. In spite of his carefully cultivated playboy reputation, he didn't take much time off. Even when he came here, he worked. Enjoying a morning at a waterfall with Hillary was an indulgence for him.

"Troy, this is incredible." Kneeling, she played her fingers through the crystal water. "I've seen infinity pools before but nothing like this one. With the way it's sunk into the balcony, it's like the pool is suspended in mid-air. What an architectural wonder. Did you come up with the design?"

"I had an idea in my mind for something like this, but I had to leave it up to the experts to make it happen. I have an architectural contact. He's more of an artist, actually."

Standing, she shook her hand dry. "One of your school pals?"

"Not this time." He slid his arm around her waist and started down the winding stairs that led from the house, down the bluff and toward the lagoon. "The architect is the stepbrother of my business partner. He had the place built from all regional materials. Most of the wood comes from Guanacaste trees…the fabrics are local weaves—"

"Whoa, hold on." She touched his stomach lightly. "You have a business partner?"

"In my software company, yes." Their flip-flops slapped each wooden plank on the way. "He provided the start-up funds."

"But I thought you came from old money? The press all said your father—" She stopped short.

"That my father bought a big company for me." He pushed past the sting of her assumption. He'd long ago accepted there were people who would always see him as a trust-fund kid. He could live with that, especially since it helped him when Salvatore needed him.

"What's the real story?"

He glanced over at her, surprised she asked. "A school friend provided an infusion of start-up cash to get things rolling. So I can't claim I did it all myself."

"I'm guessing your friend earned his money back many times over."

"Our company has done…well." Troy plucked a blue bloom from a sprawling Gallinazo tree and tucked it behind her ear.

Smiling, she touched the flower as a toucan flapped on a branch above. "You said his stepbrother designed the place. Who is this architect?"

"Jonah Landis."

"Of *the* Landis family?" Her eyebrows shot upward. "The stepbrother…is a Renshaw? Wow, you do have connections."

The Landis-Renshaw family were financial and political powerhouses. They understood his intense need to protect his privacy.

This place offered the ultimate in seclusion, with nature's soundproofing of a roaring waterfall and chattering monkeys.

His feet slowed as they reached the secluded lagoon. He set his bag on a mossy outcropping and tossed his hat on top, kicking off his sandals. He peeled his T-shirt over his head and—

Hillary stood on the edge of the shore in a bikini that glued his tongue to the roof of his mouth. Her smile was pure seduction as she backed into the water, bottle of shampoo in hand.

His erection was so damn obvious in his swim trunks, immediate, total immersion in the waterfall would be the best course of action. He climbed up the nearest rock ledge and dived in.

He parted the water with his hands, swimming closer and closer to Hillary. Her aqua-colored suit blended with the shades in the water until she appeared naked. Just what his libido needed. Yes, he wanted to seduce her. But he wanted to be in control when he did it.

Right now, he felt anything but in control.

He surfaced next to her and plucked the shampoo bottle from her hand. "Mind if I help?"

"Knock yourself out." She gave him the shampoo and disappeared underwater. The flower in her hair floated free. She shot back up again, her hair drenched and slicked back.

He squeezed shampoo in his palm then pitched the bottle back to shore. Facing her, he smoothed the shampoo along her soaked auburn locks. "How was your sister?"

The feel of her hair in his hands struck a primal chord deep inside him.

"Busy. As usual. She has the husband and kids and the big farmhouse. Our parents' old house, actually." Her head lolled back into his hands. "Where are your parents now?"

"I honestly don't know or care." His fingers clenched the rope of sudsy hair in his hands.

Her head tipped to the side as she studied him through narrowed eyes. "I didn't mean to upset you."

"Nothing upsetting about it. Just facts. You left home. So did I." Stepping behind her so she couldn't read his expression, he worked up the lather, massaging along her scalp. "Go ahead and say what you're thinking."

"I still keep in contact with my mother."

"I'm glad for you."

"I'm sorry for you. And I'm sorry I even brought this up."

"Don't be sorry." He slid his soapy hands along her shoulders, down her arms. Her silky skin sent lust throbbing through his veins, made him ache to peel away Hillary's suit and explore every soft inch of her rather than talk about his damn family. "My folks are living happily ever after, soaking in the sympathy of their friends over the huge disappointments their children have been."

"You're a billionaire, a successful software entrepreneur. You've turned your life around." She started to shift around to face him, but he stopped her, bringing her back flush against him instead. "They should be proud."

Her voice hitched, and she relaxed against him, her bottom nestled against his erection.

"I'm a self-centered playboy," he said against the top of her head, breathing in the scent of her minty shampoo. "But of course I do outscore my jailbird brother."

"What made him start using in the first place?" She reached back to cradle his cheek. "Where were your parents then? Or when he was in rehab?"

"We're adults. We take responsibility for our own actions." His heart pumped faster the harder she pushed the subject.

"But you weren't adults then."

Enough.

Enough of her trying to rationalize his past so he fit her mold of morality. He gripped her shoulders and turned her around to face him, needing her to see him, him as he really was. "We were old enough to know right from wrong and we both chose to do the wrong thing. There are consequences for that."

"Were the two of you close?" She clasped his wrists and just held on, her touch gentle but firm.

"We alternated between hating each other and being best buds. He sent me care packages at school—almost got me expelled with some of the crap he included." The memory made him smile…for a second, anyway. "I visited him in rehab to return the favor. A lot of the families there had reasons for what happened—abuse or depression leading to drug use. My brother had the same excuse I did. He was bored."

She squeezed his wrists. "I'm sorry, but I'm not letting your parents off that easily. At the very least, they were neglectful."

This conversation wasn't going the way he'd intended and this outing sure as hell wasn't going the way he'd planned.

"Troy—" she stepped closer, leaning into him "—tell me something…happy. Surely you've got some positive memories with your brother. You're a good person. I know the colonel and your brotherhood were there when you needed them, but there had to be some kind of foundation for that goodness inside you."

He wasn't sure he bought into her line of reasoning, but if it would get her smiling again, he would dig deep for something. "When we were kids, we had a nanny. When our parents weren't around we would even call her Mom."

"She sounds sweet." Hillary gifted him with a smile.

"She was tough as nails, just what two out-of-control boys needed. She was one step ahead of our pranks—and the first to reward us when we behaved."

"Reward you how?"

"Take us to baseball games, swimming at the lake, building tree houses and forts." And until now he hadn't thought about how his home here echoed those early tree houses—on a grander scale. "She even got us a couple of puppies and taught us how to take care of them."

"What kind of puppies?"

Hillary's breasts brushed his chest as they stood toe to

toe. He would keep right on happy talking for this kind of result.

"Pound puppies, of course. She told us a person's worth isn't measured by pedigree or looks. It's not about what something costs." She'd been a smart woman. He'd learned a lot from her, life lessons that stuck. "I picked a lab-bulldog mutt and my brother chose a shepherd mix."

Her smile faded. "You said you went to boarding schools, before the military school. What happened to the dogs? Did your nanny watch them?"

The water chilled around him. "When I was eight and my brother was ten, our parents fired the nanny."

"Because you were going to boarding school?"

His eyes closed. "Because they overheard us call her Mom." Her gasp pushed him to add wryly. "At least we knew she would take care of our dogs."

"Your parents gave away your dogs, too?" There was no escaping the heartbreak in her voice with just the two of them, out here alone.

He plastered on his best smile. "Damn, you asked for a happy memory. Sorry about the detour."

Sympathy shone in her eyes, along with a glint of something else. Determination. Her cool hands splayed on his chest as she stepped between his legs in a message of unmistakable seduction. "What do you say we make a great memory now?"

What the hell?

Now she wanted to make love? After he'd damn near opened a vein? Or *because* he'd opened that vein?

Realization dawned. She was feeling sorry for the kid he'd been, and was probably acting out of stirred-up emotions. He should tell her no. Wait until she was thinking clearly.

But then he'd never been particularly big on playing by the rules.

Nine

Hillary's heart was in her throat. The revelations about Troy's childhood had touched something deep inside her. She'd planned on being with him when they walked out here to the waterfall, but she'd underestimated how much he could move her. She'd deluded herself into thinking she could have a simple fling with him.

Somehow, Troy had gotten under her skin in only a few days. A few days that felt like a lifetime. She splayed her hands across his hard muscled chest sheened with water.

Troy cupped the back of her neck, his pupils dilating with arousal. "Are you seducing me?"

"Are you seducible?" She trailed her fingers down his chest.

"Totally."

He cupped her face and kissed her, openmouthed and without hesitation. She met him just as fully, wanting everything from him, determined to rock his foundation as surely as he did hers.

The taste of morning coffee lingered on his tongue. She wrapped her arms around his neck and kissed him right back, her mouth, her hands, her whole body in the moment. Finally, allowing herself to feel everything, no holding anything in reserve for later. There was no later. Everything inside her screamed *now*.

The water swirled around her, around them both, each bold caress of his hand sending the fresh currents over her. Her feet slipped on the slick stone floor and he steadied her with his hands under her bottom. The strength of his hands thrilled her. The rasp of his callused fingertips along her skin doubled the pleasure of his touch. She sketched her foot up his calf, then hooked both her legs around his waist.

The sun shone down on her head and her shoulders, but the sparks behind her eyelids had more to do with the man than the rays. And then they sank slowly underwater. Bubbles swirled around them as the rest of the shampoo left her hair. His mouth still over hers, he pumped his feet again and again, swimming backward until the suds stopped. For once, she surrendered control and let his strength carry them through the clear waters of the lagoon.

He broke the surface and she gasped for air against his shoulder. Their bodies fit, their legs brushing underwater in tantalizing swipes. She leaned into him, sealing them skin to skin.

His erection pressed against her, a solid welcome pressure against the ache building inside her. His hand braced between her shoulder blades, and she let her head fall back as he lavished attention along the exposed curves of her breasts. His mouth worked over her, teasing her through the swimsuit fabric until she reached a fever pitch.

Her hands fell away from his shoulders, and she reached behind herself. She untied the bikini strings at her neck. He smiled against her skin and made fast work of untying the rest. The scraps of aqua fabric floated away. The rippling surface brought her nipples to even tauter peaks.

He tucked an arm behind her back, tugging her hair gently until she arched farther for him, easing her breasts from the water. His mouth skimmed over one then the other, kissing and plucking as he bared her to the morning sun. He dipped his chin in the water and took her nipple lightly between his teeth, rolling and suckling, tugging just enough to send her writhing against him. Everything was brighter here, pristine when seen through the glistening droplets of water spraying from the falls. She felt like she was part of a fantasy or story or film.

From the start, she'd been drawn to Troy. They'd been leading up to this moment. Regardless of what happened afterward, she would regret it if she didn't experience today to the fullest. She wanted him inside her. Now.

She grabbed his shoulders and raised herself up again, sliding her legs to the rocky floor, pressing her body flush against his. "Do you have birth control? A condom? Because if I'm not mistaken, we're both one instant away from losing it."

"Back at the house," he murmured against her mouth. "Condoms are back at the house, damn it."

"Then we need to get there. Come on..."

He brushed his bristly, unshaven face against her cheek, whispering in her ear, "Or, we can take our time here, carefully, safely, still very pleasurably."

Possibilities swirled through her mind like the spiraling whirlpools rippling around the jutting rocks. "What exactly did you have in mind?"

He swiped his hand through the water, stirring the current between her legs until finally he cupped her. "I could touch you here." He clasped her wrist. "And if you're so inclined, you could—"

She palmed the length of his erection, stroking down, down, down and then up again, learning the thick, impressive length of him. "Is that what you mean?"

"Uh…" His head fell back and his throat moved with a slow gulp. "Yep, you're right on target."

With a deft hand, he untied the strings along her hips and the rest of her swimsuit floated away. She reached to grab it and he clasped her hand.

"I'll get you another suit just like it if you want, but right now I have more ideas for us."

His fingers slid between her legs, searching, teasing, finding the right places and pressure against the nub of nerves. Pleasure coiled tighter inside her, building. The buoyancy of the water held her up, and good thing it did, as her knees were quickly turning to jelly.

She tugged at the waistband of his trunks, her hands clumsier than she would have liked, but he was wreaking havoc with her equilibrium right now. He slid two fingers inside, crooking them just enough to send sparks exploding behind her eyelids….

To hell with taking off his shorts, she reached inside and found him, thick and long, all for her. She explored him with her hands, stroking his throbbing erection until he growled primitively in her ear. She gripped him a bit more firmly, the water slicking her hand as she worked him every bit as intensely as he tormented her. He took her to the edge, so close to fulfillment, then shifted his hands away deliberately, sipping along her neck, whispering against her skin how much he wanted her. How desperately he wanted to make her come apart, until she cried out and sank her teeth into his shoulder from the burning ache to finish.

He scooped an arm under her bottom and lifted her, walking with her toward the shore and she thought, yes, finally they would go inside and make love on his bed. Or the sofa.

Or hell, a sturdy table would suffice right now.

He kissed her, his tongue thrusting and sweeping until her eyes closed and she lost herself in the bliss of him. Step by step, he moved closer to the shoreline, until they were waist-deep in the water. His hands spanned her waist and he lifted her. She opened her eyes, disoriented, confused.

The water dripped from her skin as he set her on a moss-covered stone outcropping. He pressed her backward until she lay along the smooth, earthy rock with her legs draped over his shoulders while he still stood in the water. His intent became very clear a second before he closed his mouth over the core of her.

Her arms flung wide and dug into the mossy carpet. His tongue stroked and soothed, circling and pressing. His hands glided up her hips then over her breasts, doubling the sensation as he toyed with her. Still, she squirmed to get closer, closer still as she burned for him to finish even as she wanted the liquid fire to continue forever. Each thrum of her heart accented the pulsing pleasure growing stronger and stronger until she couldn't hold it back any longer.

She cried out her release, no holds barred. Their complete isolation gave her the freedom to ride the orgasm through each blissful aftershock. Her fingers scraped deeper into the moss, her back bowing upward as Troy laved every last sensation from her body until she collapsed, her bones all but melting into the stony outcropping.

A light breeze whispered over her bared flesh, bringing her back gust by gust. Troy lifted her off the rock and into the water again, body to body.

"Hmm…" She hummed her pleasure at this most perfect moment, but had to ask. "What about you?"

"We'll get there." Sliding an arm under her legs, he cradled her against his chest and started toward the shore. "I'm not worried."

"Where are we going?" She leaned into him, resting in his arms. Her body was all but a muscleless mass after the explosive orgasm he'd just given her.

"Back to the house before you're too sunburned to enjoy the rest of what I have planned for you."

"Smart man." She threaded her fingers through his hair, loving the length, enjoying everything about this unbelievably unique and special man.

Something insanely out of control was happening to her, and as much as she'd told herself she had crummy judgment in men, right now she felt like she'd merely been passing time until this man came into her life.

Troy carried Hillary up the winding stairs, back to the sprawling pool area. Every step he prayed for the self-control to wait until they made it back to the house. The press of her naked curves against him was damn near driving him insane with the urge to drop to the ground right here, right now and thrust inside her, out here in the open air, on the lush earth, with the scent of crushed foliage and flowers all around them.

Except he needed protection. He couldn't forget about keeping her safe in all realms. He'd stocked condoms everywhere in the house and on the patio, but he hadn't thought to pack them in their picnic lunch.

But honest to God, she'd caught him unaware down there. He'd planned to swim with her, wow her with his home. Except she'd been the one to wow him with how she'd melted over a lame story about his brother and puppies.

But then Hillary had been surprising him from the start. The only predictable thing about Hillary was her unpredictability, and for a smart guy used to figuring things out at least twenty-five steps ahead of the rest of the world, he was enjoying the hell out of the unending surprises she doled out.

And if she kept that up with her mouth on his chest, he was in danger of losing his footing, sending them both crashing down. If he rolled on the ground with her for even a second, he would lose control. Totally. Damned, though, if he could bring himself to tell her to stop what she was doing with her tongue.

Finally—thank heaven—he reached the pool area built into the balcony. He set Hillary down on a lounger, double-sized and covered by a gauzy cabana.

She reached up to cup his face. "Please say you have condoms here."

"I do." In the table by the lounger. He stretched out over her.

She skimmed her foot up and down his calf, which brought the heat of her more fully against his erection straining like hell to get out of his boxers.

"You sure were confident in your plan, Troy."

"Confident in how damned hot we both get the second you walk into the room, or into my thoughts."

"That's actually pretty romantic."

"I'm trying." Now probably wasn't the time to tell her he'd taken the edge off in the shower the night before. But he was grateful he'd done so, because no way in hell was he going to waste this chance with her on some quick trigger finish. He would be in control, damn it. Holding himself in check at the waterfall had been worth it. "And as for being confident about today? Not exactly. I'm never certain of anything around you. You surprise me on a regular basis. So while you were changing, I stored condoms in about a dozen different places."

"Why not by the waterfall—or in a beach bag for when we went to the lagoon?"

"You surprised me." And they'd improvised well.

He had no complaints about the appeal of carrying this fiery-haired beauty—*his* fiery-haired beauty—up to his lair. He was damn glad for the privacy and security that allowed him to roam the grounds freely with her. The couple who serviced the home lived five miles away, and they never came unless he called. No one would get past the wired gates without his say-so.

He and Hillary had free run to do whatever, whenever they wanted here.

"*I* surprised *you?*" She tugged the hair along his neck gently. "Very cool. Because you've been surprising the hell out of me since the second you talked your way into the seat beside me on the plane."

"Any objections?" He slipped his hand between them, gently rolling her nipple between his thumb and forefinger.

"Only that you're talking a lot, and I have better plans for your mouth right now, like using those teeth to tear into a condom wrapper."

He pressed his thigh between her legs until she moaned. "I do like a woman who knows what she wants."

"In that case, this time, I want control."

Power plays were cool by him since they were both going to be winners here. "I'm all yours."

"Well, we can start by getting rid of your board shorts." She tugged at his waistband and together they sent his swim trunks flying into the pool.

Her eyes and hands went to his hips, then curved around his arousal. He passed her one of the condoms, and she sheathed him with torturously slow precision that threatened to send him over the edge, here and now, with the monkeys laughing at his lack of restraint. But then she'd vowed this was about her turn to be in control.

Rolling with her, he shifted to his back, bringing her on top of him. She straddled his hips and lowered herself onto him inch by inch, stretching, accepting him into her body. He guided her with his hands on her hips, thrusting into her over and over as they found their rhythm. Her husky purrs of pleasure spurred him on, made him want to bring her over the edge again. He cradled her breasts, and she rewarded him with a breathy gasp. He couldn't take his eyes off the beauty of her. The way her hair slithered over her shoulders as she rode him. How her breasts moved in his hands.

The pleasure on her face.

With each stroke, he claimed her as his, again and again. Or maybe she was claiming him. Right now, all he cared about was that he had her. And he would have her over and over this week. The thought of losing this, of losing her, ripped through him, and his fingers dug into her hips, guiding her harder and faster, watching for the signals that she was close to completion, as well.

A flush rose up her chest.

The pulse in her neck throbbed faster.

Her head flung back, auburn hair streaming as she—

Yes. He thrust into her a final time, the silken vise of her body pulsing around him as he came, powerfully and completely. He pumped into her one last time and wrung yet another cry of pleasure from her. His arms went around her, gathering her as she melted onto his chest. He kissed her forehead, tasting the salty dots of perspiration along her brow. Their sweat-slicked bodies sealed and holy hell, he was in trouble.

For the past seventeen years he'd told himself he was done with family. Only claiming a group of brothers equally as cynical and world-weary as he was.

Today, with Hillary, he wanted more.

Three days later, Hillary reclined against Troy in the bubbling hot tub, mint leaves floating around them and scenting the night air. She'd had more sex since arriving here than she'd had in her entire life.

Okay, perhaps a slight exaggeration, but she certainly had never been this satisfied. Troy's meticulous attention to detail, his determination to study every possible way to make her come was mighty enticing. She'd never had a man this devoted to giving at least as much pleasure as he received. Sagging back against his chest, she let the pulsing jets work their magic on her well-loved muscles.

She tipped her head back to look at him, taking in his now-familiar face. "Thank you for my cow towel."

"You already thanked me," his voice rumbled against her.

"And for the big fuzzy cow slippers."

"Wouldn't want your feet to get cold at night." His hands slid just under her breasts, massaging her ribs, her stomach, soothing and arousing even though her body was too exhausted to comply.

"Coffee definitely tastes better in a cow mug." She twisted to kiss his shoulder, right over the spot where she'd nipped a little too hard earlier. He had a way of driving her crazy like that. "Although the hula cow by my toothbrush was a little strange, but it made me laugh."

"Then I've done my job well."

She'd laughed herself sore when she'd realized all the

computers—and there were many in his house—had Hol-stein cow screen savers.

"You've been very generous and thoughtful—and fas-cinatingly original."

"God forbid I ever be boring." His strong fingers worked along her thighs. "Would you like a black-and-white diamond pendant to go with your collection?"

"You're being outrageous." Outrageous—and so charm-ing she didn't know how she would go back to the real world again, where this fantasy would fade. Because she knew without question, the fantasy always faded.

"Damn, does that mean I have to take it back to the store?"

What was he saying? Something about a diamond cow necklace? "You didn't actually…"

"You'll have to wait and see, won't you?" His mas-saging hands slid between her legs, arousing her again after all.

As her knees eased apart, she realized the fantasy was going to live a while longer.

Troy propped his feet on his desk using an upgraded video phone that could put the competitors under if he re-leased it. He still hadn't decided.

Sometimes it was better not to upset the order of things. Leave the market alone for now and save the technology for a time it might make a significant difference rather than just adding yet another upgrade for folks to buy while tossing out products still in perfectly good working order.

All the same, he enjoyed his toys and kept the best of the best here in his own personal, techie version of a man cave. More than just a wall of computers, he had shelves of parts and storage, old and new. For now, he focused on his video call. His brother—the military school kind—

was on the other end of the conversation, still wearing his rumpled tux from the concert he'd given the night before.

"Mozart, I appreciate the help. You're the man, as always."

"It's all good, my friend." Malcolm Douglas popped an antacid in his mouth then set aside the plastic jar—already half-empty. Troy's musical protégé buddy had come a long way from his days at the military reform school—but he still had a finicky stomach. "Consider the favor done within the hour."

The casino cover story was starting to grow stale. Some might begin to suspect the truth, since Troy wasn't renowned for staying in one place for any length of time. Salvatore assured him they had leads; they were on the guy's trail, just a little longer.

But Troy wasn't willing to sit back and bet on it. Backup plans were always in order. So he'd sent photos to online magazines and gossip blogs of him with Hillary having a candlelit dinner. Spliced in with some older photos of him with Malcolm taken last month, the press and the public—and anyone else watching—would think they were in New York City, that they'd had dinner followed by attending a concert.

"Congrats on the latest gig, by the way. Not too shabby playing Carnegie Hall."

"Minor compared to what's going on in your world right now." Malcolm brushed off praise as he always had. "The new woman in your life is smokin' hot. A California dime, no doubt."

"Thanks, and careful. That's my 'ten.'"

"Hey, just sayin'." His buddy continued to push Troy's buttons for fun. It's what they did.

"Note to self, no more candlelight photos for Mozart."

Malcolm pointed. "I'm not talking about your romantic dinner pics, buddy. She's rocking the fluffy robe."

Troy spun his chair around fast, feet back on the ground. Sure enough, Hillary stood behind him in her robe, her eyes wide. "Are you talking to *the* Malcolm Douglas?"

Jealousy spiked, fast and furious and irrational. He forced himself not to go all caveman just because the woman he cared about happened to be a groupie for this generation's cross between Harry Connick Jr. and Michael Buble.

Tearing his eyes off Hillary, Troy pivoted back to the screen. "Gotta run, pal. Thanks again for the help. I owe you."

"And I will collect. Count on it."

The screen went blank.

Strolling deeper in the room, she angled her head to the side, auburn hair still tousled from sex and sleep, then more sex and sleep. "Your brothers run in high circles. The friend who helped you at the casino and now him." She gestured to the empty screen. "There sure are a lot of you."

"I wouldn't say 'a lot' of us exactly." He rocked back in his office chair. "That would make us so…cookie cutter."

"Trust me, no one would ever call you cookie cutter." She held up her hand, a platinum necklace with a white-and-black diamond cow charm dangling from her fingers. "You are one hundred percent original."

He grabbed her wrist and tugged her into his lap. "Now that is the hottest thing you've ever said to me."

"I must not be holding up my end of the seduction then." She wriggled in his lap until she settled.

"You're killing me here. I need an energy drink."

"Which I'll be happy to get for you if you'll make me one promise."

"What's that?"

"I adore the necklace and gladly accept it. But from here on out, dial back on the extravagant gifts. Okay?"

"Fair enough."

He slid the necklace from her hand. He swept aside her hair and hooked the chain around her neck. He might not be the most romantic guy in the world, but he prided himself on his originality, and he would do everything in his power to obliterate the memory of Barry Curtis.

He pressed a kiss to the latched chain.

She glanced back at him, their mouths and eyes so close they almost touched. "What are you thinking?"

"Something a smart man wouldn't say." A wry smile tugged at him.

"What do you mean?"

"Why would you want to know if I've already warned you it might upset you?" Standing, he set her on her feet, cow slippers poking out from the hem of her robe.

"Because…" She tugged his T-shirt holding him closer. "If you really didn't want me to know, you would have said something like…'nothing' or 'I'm thinking about breakfast or what goofy hat I'm going to buy next.'"

"You think my hats are goofy?"

"I'll answer you if you answer me."

Ah, what the hell? Might as well. "I was thinking about you and your jackass of an ex-boyfriend. I was wondering if you're still in love with him."

Whoa? Wait. That wasn't exactly what he'd been thinking. He'd just wanted to be sure she was over him. The *love* word hadn't entered his mind. But now that he'd gone there with the conversation, there was no going back.

She sank down into his empty chair, confusion on her face as she studied him. "Looking back, I can see I was never in love with him. I was definitely infatuated—very infatuated." She grimaced, fingering the diamond necklace. "Dazzled a little. But I like to think I would have seen through the glitz to the real guy underneath at some point."

He leaned back against a table of surveillance proto-types, listening. Hoping for what, he wasn't sure.

"What can I say?" She shrugged. "I told you right from the start that I have a history for picking bad guys. Eventually, I figure it out. In this case, Barry's arrest just sped up the realization process."

Usually he rocked at being analytical underneath all the jokes, but right now it was tougher than usual. Still, he forced himself to sift through the words. She didn't love Barry Curtis.

"Okay, then. I can live with that."

Too bad one realization led to another. She doubted her ability to choose the right guy to love, period.

Leaning her elbows on her knees, she pinned him with her eyes. "How can you be jealous when you've only known me a few days?"

"Who says I'm jealous?" Lame answer for a smart dude.

"Really? You want to try and bluff?" She laughed... then realized her robe was gaping. She straightened fast and held the part closed. She was shutting down and if he didn't do or say something fast, he could lose headway in his goal of... What?

He knew damn well what. It didn't matter how long he'd known her. He was certain. He wanted her in his life. Permanently. But he wasn't sure she was ready to hear that yet. She might not have loved Barry, but she'd been burned badly by the relationship.

The timing needed to be right. He couldn't afford to screw this up.

So he shoved away from the table and stalked toward her, at least letting all the possessive feelings show. "I'm not jealous so much as pissed off that the bastard hurt you."

He pressed his hands on either side of the chair, bringing their faces nose to nose. "I want to beat the crap out of him then hack his identity and wreck his credit. Got a problem with that?"

A slow smile spread over her face. "No problem at all." She tugged his bottom lip between her teeth. "And just so we're totally clear, I think your hats are sexy as hell."

Ten

Her time here was surely coming to a close.

Hillary floated on a raft, warm waters of the infinity pool lapping over her. She watched Troy swim the length of the pool. Lights underwater illuminated him powering through the depths, while the stars twinkled above on a cloudless night.

She and Troy had all but lived outside and at the lagoon since they'd arrived five days ago. They'd taken walks—made love in the forest—shared exotic delicacies—made love in the cabana. Learned personal details from political views to a shared preference for scary movies. Eventually they'd made their way inside to dodge the rain, enjoying a horror film in the theater-style screening room.

Like a real date.

But real life intruded often enough to keep her from getting too comfortable, too complacent, too eager to believe in something beyond the fantasy. Daily calls from

Salvatore let them know he was getting closer. Barry Curtis's accomplice had been tracked slipping over the channel into Belgium. They were on his tail and expected to catch him at any time.

What amazed her most was how easily Troy and Salvatore had maneuvered this whole situation while keeping things anonymous. Calls from her sister indicated the public was eating up tabloid stories of Hillary and Troy gallivanting around the globe, wining and dining in a different country every night.

While she'd enjoyed their dinner in France, she had to admit, the time alone with him was more precious.

Troy surged to the surface beside her. "Hey, beautiful." He lifted her hand and kissed each fingertip. "We're going to be waterlogged by the time we leave this place."

"Is that a bad thing?" Especially given the attention he was lavishing on her hand at the moment.

"Not at all." He rested his elbows on the edge of her raft. "Just checking to make sure you're cool with how little time we've spent in an actual bed."

He'd been attentive, romantic, and she was so tempted to think there was more going on here. But she needed to remember this would end soon. Life back in D.C.—in the real world—would be different. It always was. Still, she would miss the peacefulness of this place.

She toyed with his hair, longer now that it was wet. "Sleeping in the cabana was romantic. And watching the sunrise on the balcony—amazing. The past five days have been better than any vacation I could imagine. You've got the perks of this place down to an art."

"An art? What do you mean?" He trailed the backs of his fingers along her breast, down her side and over her bare hip. They'd never gotten around to putting on clothes today.

She was totally naked other than wearing her diamond cow necklace.

"If you've never brought anyone here, where did you romance all those women you were linked with in the tabloids?" She hated the hint of jealousy leaking into her tone regardless of how hard she tried to tamp it down.

"Are you jealous?"

Hell, yes. "Curious."

"Everything in the tabloids? All false." His face was stamped with deep sincerity. "I was a virgin until I met you."

Snorting on a laugh, she rolled her eyes. "Right."

"Serious," he continued, with overplayed drama. "I've lived like a monk. My staff put saltpeter in all my drinking water so I could save myself until the day I met you."

She splashed him in the face. "You're outrageous."

"So you've told me." He snagged her hand before she could splash him again, his face truly earnest now. "Would you rather I detailed past affairs? Because that's all they were. Affairs. Not relationships. Not serious. And never permanent."

Her stomach fluttered at the turn in the conversation. "Is that what we're doing here? Having an affair?"

"Damned inconvenient time for an affair, if you ask me."

"Okay then, are we having an inconvenient affair?" Those butterflies worked overtime, so much so she couldn't even pretend she didn't care about his answer.

"What if I said this isn't an affair?" He pinned her with his eyes as they floated together in the center of the pool. "I saw you, and I had to have you."

The possessive ring in his voice carried on the wind. Exciting in some ways, and perhaps a hint Cro-Magnon in others.

"That sounds more like I was a piece of cheesecake on a tray at a restaurant."

He winked. "I do like cheesecake."

"Could you be serious?" She flicked a light spray into his face.

He tugged her in with him, and they pushed away from the float. Sliding deeper into the pool, she treaded water, face-to-face with Troy. She looped her arms around his neck and their feet worked below the surface keeping them both afloat.

"Do you want me to be serious?" His hands cupped her bottom, their bodies a seamless fit against each other. "Because I can be, very much so. Except I get the sense that the timing is off, and if I tell you exactly what I'm thinking, you'll run."

His perceptiveness surprised her. She'd spent so much time enjoying his lighthearted ways and trying to remind herself this was a fantasy that would end, she hadn't considered he might be thinking of more after this week.

And he was one hundred percent right that the thought of life after Costa Rica scared her. "You're a very wise man."

Disappointment flickered through his eyes for an instant before his easygoing smile returned. "Then let's get back to having an inconvenient affair."

He sidestroked them to the edge of the pool. Her back met the tiled wall where his feet just touched the ground. He kissed her neck in the sensitive crook, paying extra attention to the place just below her ear that made her...*sigh*.

The hard muscles of his chest pressed to her breasts. Heat tingled through her veins, surging and gathering low. She explored the planes of his shoulder blades, his broad shoulders and his arms that held her so securely. He hitched her legs around his waist and started walking toward the semicircle of concrete stairs, kissing her every step of the way.

Climbing the stairs, still he held her. The air washed over their damp bodies. Goose bumps rose along her skin, every bit as much from Troy as from the night air. She tangled her fingers in his hair, loving the unconventional, uncut look of him.

With her legs looped around his waist, he carried her into the spacious house. Through the living area where they'd made love on a chaise lounge with the windows open. Past the kitchen counter where they'd had breakfast and each other. And down the hall to his bedroom where they'd yet to spend a night under the covers together.

He lowered her onto the towering carved bed draped with mosquito netting, like another tree house inside the ultimate tree house. The rest of the room was sparse, with only a wardrobe and a mammoth leather chair by the window. He presented such a fascinating mix of wealth and Spartan living.

But right now, she didn't want to think about his decor. Only feel. "This whole week has been a fantasy."

"You like fantasies?"

"What exactly do you have in mind?"

He eased back to his feet and went to the wardrobe. He tugged out his tuxedo jacket and shook it. Something rattled in the pocket. He pitched the jacket to her and she fished inside to find...

"Handcuffs?" She spun them on a finger. "Do you carry these around as a regular accessory?" Her mind filled with sensual possibilities, games she would only play with someone she trusted, and yes, at some point she'd learned to trust him. A scary thought, if she let herself ponder it for too long. So she again focused on the moment, on Troy and on the pleasure they were going to give each other very, very soon.

"They're from when I was auctioned off. I tucked them in my pocket and forgot about them until you mentioned fantasies." He closed the wardrobe, the dim lamplight casting a warm glow over his lean naked body. "The cuffs would have ended up at the cleaners when my tuxedo went in to be dry-cleaned, but we rushed out of the hotel so fast I never got around to it."

"The bachelor auction and the way you turned it around was quite a stunt." She'd been drawn to him then, in spite of her frustration over how little he'd told her on the plane.

He knelt on the edge of the bed, moving up the mattress until he covered her. "The auction was uncomfortable as hell, but it worked out well."

"I have to confess…" She stroked back his still-damp hair, the scent of mint and furniture polish riding the humid air. "I was jealous of your assistant, before I knew who she was, when I thought she'd won a weekend with you."

"Jealous, huh?" He hooked two fingers in the other side of the cuff, tugging lightly. "Feel free to elaborate."

"I was hoping plastic surgery chick would win."

"She wouldn't have," he said confidently. A drop of water from his wet hair spilled on her overheated flesh, trickling between her breasts.

Her nipples tightened from just that one droplet. She shivered in anticipation of how much more there was in store for them.

"The bidding could have gone much higher."

"I still would have won." His eyes blazed with flinty determination. "My assistant was authorized to do whatever it took."

"Just so you could choose me?" How far would he have gone?

"I didn't believe Salvatore was doing enough to protect you." He linked fingers with her, the handcuffs clasped in their joined hands. "I had to come up with a way to keep watch over you and that seemed the easiest way."

His words about safety chilled her, reminding her of their reason for being here in the first place. While she didn't doubt he was attracted to her, would they have ended up here on their own? Would he have pursued her had he just met her on the street? Old insecurities niggled.

"Spending eighty-nine-thousand dollars was easy?" She attempted to hide her unease with a joke like he did so often. "Why not hire a bodyguard? It would have been cheaper."

"You know how you said you were jealous of my assistant?" He held both her hands, pressing them into the mattress, his erection thick against her stomach. "I felt the same at the thought of turning you over to some security guy."

She arched up into him, enjoying the heat flaming hotter in his eyes. The scent of native flowers drifted on the breeze through the open windows, providing an intoxicating moment when she realized just how aware she was around this man.

A sense of power pulsed through her, and she embraced it, needing to feel in control of something here. "The attraction between us was pretty instantaneous."

"Once the auction rolled around, I was so damn happy to see you out there in the audience." He grinned down at her. "And then I was so turned on I had to keep my hands in front of me."

Now that would have made headlines. "I thought that was just because of the handcuffs."

"Oh, it was the handcuffs all right." He squeezed her hand in his, still holding the handcuffs. "Thinking about ways that you and I could use them had me sweating bullets. Which brings us back to fantasies."

"You've had fantasies, about me and handcuffs?" The simmering heat inside her flamed to life. "What exactly would you like to do with those handcuffs?"

"I wouldn't want to shock a Vermont farm girl."

"Please…" She tugged the handcuffs from him and dangled them in front of his face. "Shock me."

Troy had never been one to turn down a challenge.

And the challenge in Hillary's eyes was one he very much looked forward to fulfilling. He snapped one cuff around her right wrist and the other around his left, so they were shackled while facing each other. The past five days with Hillary had been beyond incredible, and with time running out, he hoped he could cement their bond before they left.

She blinked up at him in surprise. "I thought you were going to cuff me to the bed, Viking style."

"Then I did surprise you." He sketched his hand along her breast, which brought her hand to herself, as well.

She slid her free hand between them to stroke him but he manacled her wrist and pinned it against the bed.

"Troy," she said, writhing against him, the ache inside her building, "I want to touch you, too."

"We'll get around to that. We have all night." And if he had his way, they would have even longer.

"Who says you get to be in control?" She pressed back, knowing there was no way she could actually win in a contest of pure muscle, but maybe she had a chance in the battle of wills. "My. Turn."

He laughed softly against her, the puff of air along her

breasts sending fresh shivers down her spine. Then he rolled to his back, taking her with him. "Consider me at your command."

Her smile of pure feminine power launched a fresh flood of testosterone pounding through him in answer. Her hands still linked with his, she kissed her way over his chest, lingering and laving her way down until…holy crap, her lips closed around him. His head dug back into the pillow as he lost himself in the moist and warm temptation of her mouth, the tempting sweep of her tongue. She shouldn't be able to take him to the edge so fast, but then nothing was as he expected with Hillary.

The only thing he knew for sure was that he didn't want this to end.

He tugged their cuffed wrists and hauled her upward, unyielding, and flipped her to her back again, the length of him pressed between her legs. The silky dampness of her let him know she was every bit as ready as he was. With his free hand, he tugged on a condom in record time and slid into her welcoming heat. He knew her body after all they'd done together, yet still he couldn't get enough of her. Of the soaring sensation of being inside her with the scent of their mutual arousal perfuming the air.

The link between them was real, damn it. Every bit as real as the handcuffs binding them together. She had to see that, to believe it. He just needed to be patient and work past her insistence that her judgment in men was off. He needed to win her trust.

She hooked her ankles behind his back and took him deeper inside her, rolling her hips and bringing them both closer to completion. He wanted to wait—he had to wait—for her. Gritting his teeth, he held back his release, until finally, thank heaven, her breath hitched with the special sound that preceded her…cries of completion.

His own control snapped and he thrust again deeper, shouting with his own release jetting through him. Again. And again. Until he sagged on top of her, just barely managing to hold the bulk of his weight off her by levering on his elbows. He rolled to his side, their hands still locked together. He flung his other arm over his eyes, his defenses stripped back until he was unable to hide from the secret he'd been holding all day.

Salvatore had called after supper. Barry Curtis's accomplice had been picked up trying to slip into Switzerland. Extradition was already underway.

Hillary was cleared to return to D.C.

While the morning sun climbed, Hillary rested her chin on her hands on Troy's chest. The handcuffs rested on the pillow beside her. She would have to remember to tuck them away to play with again on another day. The whole Viking scenario held a certain appeal.

She kissed his chin. "You most definitely are not a monk."

"Nice to know you noticed," he said, his fingers tracing lazy circles on her back. "Have you checked under your pillow?"

Her hand went to her diamond necklace then over to her pillow. She tumbled underneath and her fingers closed around... Metal? She closed her fist around something square and pulled out...

"A cowbell?" Laughing, she rolled to her back, clanging the copper bell.

"Everything's better with a little cowbell."

"I can't believe you got this."

He rolled to his side, eyes on her face intensely, like he was looking for something. "You said I couldn't buy you extravagant gifts, so I've been working within your system."

"It's sweet. Really." She kissed him quickly. "I can honestly say I have never gotten one before."

"What till you hear my cow jokes. What do you call a sleeping cow?"

"A bull dozer."

"Okay, too easy." He threw a leg over hers, the ceiling fan stirring the mosquito netting. "Mooo-ving on."

She groaned.

"Why do milking stools only have three legs? Because the cow has the udder."

She swatted him with a pillow, the cuffs clattering to the floor. "That's awful."

"I know. I went through a lot of corny jokes at school until I learned the nuances of humor."

Something shifted inside her at those words, at the image of him "learning" to be funny, trying to fit in as he was tossed from school to school, his parents abdicating their roles in his life.

He flung his arms wide. "What? You don't have any ammo to toss back? Roll out the computer geek jokes. Take your best shot. I'm bulletproof. More than that, I'm a bullet catcher."

"You're a cocky bastard." But she sensed he hadn't always been that way. But saying as much would take them to a serious level she wasn't ready for, not yet. So she scrounged for a joke…. "Ethernet—something to catch the Ether Bunny."

"Oh," he groaned. "Talk about bad. You're a rookie."

She pushed for more, determined to keep it light and make the most of their time here before he told her they had to leave. "The truth is out there…if only I had the URL."

"Better."

"There are ten types of people. The ones who understand binary code and the ones who don't."

"Ahh," he said as he sighed, pulling her close. "Now you're making me hot."

She splayed her fingers over his chest, traced four scratch marks she'd left earlier. "You're crazy."

"That's very possible."

A darkness in his eyes unsettled her. "I was joking."

"I wasn't. This genetic lottery thing…" He tapped his temple. "It's enabled me to do some incredible things with my life. But sometimes it fails me on the basic things in life, things that everyone else has and takes for granted."

So much for staying away from deeper subjects. She should have known there was no hiding, especially not with Troy. And she found she actually wanted to know. She needed to understand him. "Such as?"

"A family. One that functions and talks to each other and eats Sunday dinners together."

"Troy," she gasped, gripping his shoulders insistently. "You can't blame yourself for your family friction."

"I played my part. You know, I could have just sucked it up and gone to medical school like my father wanted. It wouldn't have been that difficult for me academically," he said with confidence but not arrogance. He hooked his finger in her necklace, sliding it back and forth. "I could have done some kind of research gig where I wouldn't be around people."

God, he was breaking her heart here. "I don't know where in hell you got this idea that you're not good with people. You're charming and funny." She covered his hand on her necklace. "A total original."

"Like I said, it's a game I learned and I'm cool with that."

"Not a game." She shook her head. "I think maybe you learned to share parts of yourself, in a way others can understand."

She pressed her mouth to his before he could argue with her, her heart tumbling over itself with love for this man and sadness that she would soon have to leave him behind.

Eleven

Troy stood on the balcony, cell phone to his ear, trying to outtalk the monkeys and birds yammering in the trees. "Thanks for the update, Colonel. Glad to know Curtis is finally spilling his guts."

"It's a race between the two to make a deal. International money laundering doesn't sit well with the authorities. And stealing from disadvantaged kids' college scholarship funds plays even worse in the press." Salvatore's heavy sigh carried through the airwaves. "When are you and Hillary Wright coming in this morning?"

"Not this morning. But soon." When he got around to telling her.

"Donavan," the colonel said in the suspicious headmaster tone he'd honed over the years. "You've informed Hillary that all's clear. Right?"

"Of course I will, tonight." He leaned back against the rail, splinters snagging on his board shorts.

"Ah, Donavan." Salvatore all but tut-tutted at him. "How can a man so smart be so damn stupid?"

"Thanks for the vote of confidence, sir." Troy gripped the balcony harder, splinters digging straight into his palms. "If that's all, how about you roll me to the bottom of your on-call list?"

Salvatore's mocking laugh faded as Troy hit the end call button and set the cell on the rail.

Time was running out. Even the cackling monkeys in the trees seemed to be mocking him for being an idiot. Salvatore was right; he couldn't keep Hillary here indefinitely. He would take her home and just ask her out like a regular guy once they returned to the States.

Except he'd never done the "regular guy" gig all that well.

He heard Hillary's near-silent footsteps approaching a few seconds before she placed her hand in the middle of his back, her fingers curving in with familiarity.

"Was that good news on the phone?"

"Yeah…" He looked down at the lagoon where he'd made love to Hillary for the first time. Would she come back here or was this some fantasy escape for her, one that would be over and done when she was back home? He would tell her after lunch. She would still be back before the end of her hastily scheduled vacation. He needed to use this last pocket of time to seal the deal. "Work stuff. Mergers. Money. Boring office crap."

Hillary slid in front of him, wearing a floral sarong knotted over her breasts, a flower tucked behind her ear. She had sun-kissed cheeks and an ease to her that hadn't been there before they'd come here. When they returned, would she wear those buttoned-up suits like armor to keep him out?

"I would think you'd be happy." She sketched her fingers over his forehead. "You look worried."

"I am happy." He nodded, trying to shake the whole gloom-and-doom air weighing down his mojo. What the hell was up with that? He was the guy of the fedora hats and cool scarves.

She toyed with the string on his board shorts. "Let's take brunch up to the roof today. I think it's the only place where we haven't made love yet."

The vision of her with the waterfall in the background, mist in the air, wild outdoors all around them, took his breath away. He couldn't lose her. He needed to bind her to him before they left, ensure they had a future.

"Do you ever think about having kids?"

Hillary leaned back, her eyes wide. "Are you trying to tell me the condom broke?"

"No! God, no." Although the thought of a kid with Hillary didn't scare him as much as it should.

A sigh moved visibly through her. "Then that seems to be a rather premature question." She slid her arms around his waist. "Shouldn't we figure out if we're going to see each other after we leave here?"

"Lady, that's a given." At least he hoped it was. And if not, he intended to make it one. "And as for the kid question, I didn't say *our* kids, I said kids. Period. When people date—like we're talking about doing when we get back to the States—then they discuss their views on life stuff. Like having children."

"Okay," she said slowly, her voice wary, "then yes, sometimes I think about it."

"And your verdict?"

Why the hell had that jumped out of his mouth now? Her answer mattered to him, more than he was comfortable with. He was supposed to be romancing her to seal the deal, not freaking her out with a full-court press.

"Honestly, Troy, the thought scares the hell out of me. What do I know about being a mom?" She spread her arms wide before tapping his chest. "And you mentioned genetics once. What about that? What if between our genes and the patterns we've seen, our kids… I mean… Ah, hell." She shoved against his chest. "Why are you bringing this up now? We should be talking about whether to go out for pizza or steak."

He shifted away from her, leaning back against the balcony. "I always thought I would adopt."

His answer stopped her. She turned to face him again. "Really?"

"Sure, once I found the right woman to spend my life with, because I don't know that I'm up to the task of parenting alone."

"And you would adopt because of the genetics fears you talked about?"

"In part, maybe. But I also figure I have all of this money and flexibility and there are kids out there without homes. Maybe I could just say to hell with worrying about someone getting into trouble and go ahead and adopt a troubled kid. Help them turn it around, give a kid the same break I got."

"You would do that?" She came back to him, leaning a hip against the rail. "Take in a child you already knew had problems?"

"If I had a biological kid who got into trouble like me and my brother did, I wouldn't just write him or her off." Memories of fights with his dad reverberated in his head. "And by problems, maybe I would take in a kid with medical problems, someone overlooked. I could pay for anything that kid needed. And hats. Lots of little hats for the kid."

Her eyes welled with tears as she touched his cheek. "Are you for real? Or is this an act to make women love you?"

"Would you believe me even if I said every word is true?"

He pushed back a wince at how he'd delayed for a day in telling her they could leave Costa Rica. He hadn't lied, he'd just...

Quibbled.

That's what Hillary would call it, and she wouldn't be forgiving of what she considered a lie. But how could he let her go not knowing if she'd agree to see him again?

"The thought of believing everything you're saying scares me. The fantasy is so much easier." She pulled a wobbly smile. "Even with the handcuffs."

"You're worried I'll hurt you." Even the thought of anyone hurting her made him want to haul her in and hold her tight.

"Remember when we talked about your happy childhood memory?" She folded her arms over her chest. "When my sisters and I were little, we would ride around on the tractor with Dad. He told us we were princesses and that was our chariot. It was fun to pretend."

"If you loved the farm so much, why were you so hungry to leave?"

"Because I realized all those times on the 'chariot'— that was just to protect the queen while she was toasted." She wrapped her arms around herself tighter, all but putting a wall between them.

"He was protecting his kids, you mean," he said, trying to put a positive spin on things, to give her something happier to hold on to.

"If he'd been protecting us, he wouldn't have enabled her. He loved her, but he was scared of her. He was scared if he pressed her to change, she would leave him." She stopped and held up her hand. "Whoa. Wait. I screwed up that happy memory exchange, too. Anyhow, I left the farm, but I don't hate it. I still go back to visit—my sister lives there with her family now that our dad's gone. Mom lives in an apartment—when she's not in rehab."

To hell with distance. He hauled her against his chest again. "I'm sorry for all you've been through. I can see how that would make you wary. But you can trust me, Hillary—"

His cell rang on the porch railing.

She looked quickly at the phone. "You should get that."

"Ignore it."

"It could be important."

Sighing, he snatched up the damn phone, knowing she was right. His assistant's name scrolled across the caller ID. If this had anything to do with Hillary's safety, he couldn't afford to ignore it.

"What?" he barked into the phone, resenting the intrusion of the outside world. "This better be important."

"It is. Hillary Wright's sister is going crazy trying to get in touch with her. Says it's something to do with their mother."

In the privacy of her room, Hillary cradled the phone and dialed her sister. After the intense conversation with Troy, she needed her space to face a call about her mother.

Why in the world did he have to bring up kids now? So early in their relationship? She was still adjusting to being in love with him. And then he had to roll out those incredibly enticing images of him as a dad, of him opening his life and heart to a kid who desperately needed a family. He was making her think he might want a future with her. Had she willingly signed on for another heartbreak by coming here with him?

The ringing in the phone receiver stopped and her youngest niece started chattering into the phone, "Aunt Hillary, Aunt Hillary, Grandma's moving in with us!"

Shock froze her. Her sister had always been softer where their mother was concerned, but she couldn't have actually caved on this. What about the children? "Could you please put your mommy on the phone?"

"Okeydokey. Love you, Aunt Hillary."

She clutched the phone tighter. "Love you, too, sweetie. See you when you come to Washington for your family vacation."

The sound of her niece shouting, "Mommm, telephone, Aunt Hillary," sounded in the background. Footsteps grew louder, then the rustling of the phone being passed over.

"Hillary?" her sister gasped into the phone.

"Claudia, what is going on there? I got an emergency SOS to call and now I hear Mom's moving in with you. Are you nuts?" All her fears and frustrations poured out in nervous babbling. "This is taking the codependent thing a little far, don't you think? You can't really expect to have her there with your children, can you? Maybe you don't remember what it was like, but I do."

"Hillary," Claudia interrupted. "Slow down, okay? I need to tell you something and it's a tough one."

"I'm already sitting." But she scooted farther back on the bed, nerves frothing in her stomach. "What's wrong?"

"While Mom was in the rehab clinic, the doctors found out she has a mass on her liver…." Claudia paused, her voice catching. "It's cancer, Hillary, and it's bad. End stage. The doctors say she has a couple of months left, tops. Her apartment isn't an assisted living type of setup. She has nowhere else to go."

Shock numbed Hillary as she absorbed the last thing she'd expected to hear. She'd spent her whole life figuring out how to cope with having an alcoholic mother. She'd never thought about how to cope with not having her mother at all. "I'm coming to Vermont."

"You don't have to rush right away—"

"Yes, I believe I do." She leaped from the bed, trying to deny the voice whispering in her mind that she wasn't running to her mother.

She was running away from Troy and the fear of him rejecting her love.

Troy stood in the open doorway of Hillary's room watching her pace frantically around, throwing clothes into her suitcase. From her tense shoulders to the sheen of tears in her eyes, he knew.

"I assume it was bad news on the phone."

She nodded tightly, folding her cow towel quickly and pressing it on top of everything else in her roller bag. "It is." She sat on the case and zipped. "My mother is ill, very ill. She has liver cancer. She doesn't have long left. I need to go home now and help my sister get Mom's affairs in order. We have to set up hospice, so many details."

She ticked through the to-do list efficiently. Even in a sarong, she could still harness the buttoned-up suit-type organization. She all but wrapped herself in competence.

"Oh God, Hillary." He pushed away from the door, reaching for her. "I'm sorry. Is there something I can do to help? Doctors? Specialists?"

She stopped in her tracks. "Actually, I do need something. I need for you to be sure my family won't be in any kind of danger if I'm there."

Ah, hell. She thought they still had to hide out here, away from Barry Curtis's accomplice. He could almost hear Salvatore's mocking laughter in his ears, followed by an *I told you so* for not letting Hillary in on the news sooner.

He took her hands in his. "No worries on that front. Actually, we're cleared to leave anytime."

"Really? Did they catch the mystery guy we identified in the surveillance footage?" Confusion chased across her face. "Are we sure there won't be retaliation against us for making the identification?"

"They have him in custody. Barry Curtis is talking now. They are in a rush to outconfess each other, so Interpol doesn't need our testimony." And he was damn grateful he didn't need to worry about her safety, although he knew now he would never stop being concerned for her. "We're just icing on the cake for them."

"That's awesome, and crazy convenient in the timing." She pressed a hand to her forehead, then, slowly, realization dawned in her eyes. "That call this morning, the good news, it wasn't about work was it? It was Salvatore."

"Yes, it was." He couldn't deny it.

"Why didn't you tell me? When did he find out?"

He hesitated a second too long.

Disillusionment flooded her face, followed by anger. "You knew before this morning, didn't you?"

Resolution settled deep in his gut, along with the urge to kick himself for being worse than an idiot. "I heard late yesterday afternoon."

"Why? Why wouldn't you tell me?" Pain laced her every word. "Why would you let me worry and wonder? It's almost like you kidnapped me, handcuffing me here with a lie."

"I intended to tell you today. I just wanted to enjoy a final night with you."

"That wasn't your decision to make." Her eyes went cynical as she backed away. "But then maybe you already knew that. Consciously or subconsciously, you sabotaged this relationship because you don't want the reality, just this tree house fantasy."

"Damn it, Hillary, that's not true. Give me a chance to explain." He gripped her by the shoulders.

But her body was like ice under his hands.

"I only have one question for you, Troy." She met his gaze unflinchingly, beautiful and so vulnerable. "Why couldn't you have just been honest with me? Why did you have to go to such lengths to break my heart?"

Her words stabbed him clean through. He'd vowed over and over that his intent was to protect her and yet he'd done the thing guaranteed to hurt her most. There wasn't any excuse he could make. No matter how much he'd worked on his people skills, he hadn't learned all the lessons he needed now.

She shrugged free of his hands. "That's what I thought. There's nothing left to say." She unhooked the diamond charm necklace and dropped it in his palm. "Please, just take me to Vermont and then get out of my life."

Twelve

She'd come full circle.

Locking her rental car, she strode up the flagstone walkway leading to her childhood home, her body more than a little weary from her day of travel, her argument with Troy. After they'd fought, he shut down. He'd offered her his plane to see her mother and then he'd disappeared into his computer-filled man cave.

And now she was home. The countryside was dark, other than lights on the house and barn and another marking the entrance to the dirt driveway.

But even in the dim light, she knew her way by heart. Her sister hadn't changed much on the two-story clapboard farmhouse, not even the black shutters. There were a few extra flowers in the garden and more toys in the yard— a bike lying on its side, tire swings spinning in the wind, and a fort built into the V of a sprawling oak tree. A sign hung on the front with *No Boys Allowed* painted in bright red letters.

Not a bad idea.

She couldn't get past feeling like a fool. After telling herself a million times Troy was a playboy and she had a radar finely tuned to find jerks, she'd still made the same mistake. She'd trusted the wrong guy.

But damn, he was so good at the game. He'd romanced her in a way no man had even thought of trying, dazzling her with contrasts. One day they were dining in France and another day picnicking off fresh fruit from the trees around his Costa Rican retreat. Who gave a woman a cowbell as well as a charm with exclusive black diamonds?

A genius playboy, that's who. He'd told her he'd studied how to be funny, how to charm and weave his way through society, yet somehow she'd never considered he was using those skills to manipulate her into going to bed with him in less than a week. She wanted to pound her head against a tree.

Or collapse on the front stoop and cry her eyes out.

Her older sister pushed through the front screen door, hinges creaking. They could have been twins born seven years apart, yet they'd taken two such different paths. As much as Hillary had scoffed at anyone staying on this farm, her sister definitely appeared to be the wiser one.

Claudia opened her arms and hugged her hard. They'd been close as kids, taking care of each other. What had changed? When had she quit helping her sister?

Hillary stepped back and hooked an arm with Claudia. "Where are the kids and hubby?"

"Asleep, but looking forward to seeing you in the morning. Where's your Robin Hood Hacker Hunk?"

"Long story. Can we save it for later?" When she could talk about him without crying? Like maybe sometime in

the next decade. "I'm sorry to have kept you up so late…
I'm sorry I left you to take care of everything with Mom
and Dad."

"You don't have to apologize for anything." Claudia
squeezed her sister's hand on their way up the steps they'd
climbed countless times. "You're living your life. That's
what grown-ups are supposed to do."

"Are you living yours the way you want? With Mom
staying here?" She needed to hear that she hadn't totally
wrecked her sister's life by bailing.

Claudia tugged open the creaky screen again. "No one
wants to have an alcoholic mother in and out of rehab clin-
ics. And I'm sure you don't want to have to keep footing
the bill because I'm too cash-strapped with three kids to
feed. We both do what we can."

"Writing the check is easy."

"Ha! So says the woman who doesn't have a kid in
braces." Her sister guided her through the house, toward the back guest room. "Come on. Mom tried to stay
awake to see you, but she's on a lot of pain medication.
She drifted off about an hour ago."

Only a few more steps and they would be outside their
mother's door, where she slept.

"I'll see her in the morning then. We could all use a
good night's sleep." Hillary turned quickly, stopping in
the kitchen, a traditional wide-open space with a six-seat
oak table in the middle. "I appreciate your trying to make
the distribution seem fair, but I still feel guilty. Like I've
run away."

"We're both children of an alcoholic. That leaves a
mark on the way we deal with things." Claudia snagged
a caffeine-free Diet Coke off the counter, popped the top
and passed it to her sister before getting one for herself. "I
lean toward the whole codependent gig, and you lean to-

ward avoidance. We're both trying to do better, to be better. I figure as long as we're both still trying, then there's nothing to be gained from beating up on ourselves."

Hillary leaned against the tile counter, sipping the Diet Coke. "It seems so strange that she came here to die when she always swore she hated this place, that the boredom drove her to drink."

"Honey," her sister crooned squeezing her arm, "you gotta know that was just an excuse."

Hillary looked around the kitchen with all its windows showcasing the wide-open space…much like Troy's place. "It's really pretty here."

"Yes, it is." Her sister smiled serenely, tipping back her can of soda.

"You can say 'I told you so' if you want." She deserved everything coming her way after she'd been all but snobby about the place. Until this moment, she'd never really seen her home without the dark filter of her mom's bitterness.

"I'm not a gloater. You should know that about me." Her sister tapped her can against Hillary's.

"I do, which is probably why I offered to let you lord it over me, since I knew you wouldn't."

"That's convoluted logic."

"I picked it up from the best." Another thing she'd learned from Troy this week. How could so much happiness and pain be mingled together?

Her sister cocked her head to the side, brow furrowed. "You can love here and love somewhere else, too. That's okay."

Hillary nodded. "I'm starting to understand that." She looked around at the children's art on the fridge, at the cow clock on the wall, and found the words falling from her mouth in spite of the burn of tears behind her eyes. "Troy has this place in Costa Rica, and it's amazing. But not because it's flashy. His home is actually very rustic—with a lot of high-tech gadgetry of course, but the look of the place is earthy. It's *real*."

"Sis, I gotta confess, this is a stretch. You're comparing Costa Rica with Vermont? No offense to my beloved home state, of course."

"I know, I know, I've thought the same thing." Her jumbled thoughts from this whole crazy week started coming together in her mind like puzzle pieces.... She'd been using the farm as an excuse for her own unhappiness. On some level, she must have known that or why else would she have insisted on carrying little cow talismans as reminders of home? Her childhood hadn't been perfect, but it hadn't been all bad. There were good memories, too. Life wasn't clear-cut or black-and-white like the spots on a cow.

Had she been missing the boat on her career, as well? Focusing on the glitz at the expense of depth? Did she really want to spend the rest of her life planning parties? Troy had found simplicity and meaning underneath all the wealth. She'd been so busy judging Troy, she hadn't considered her own superficial choices. Her narrow view of the world had likely led to her previous bad choices in men.

But she should have realized Troy was different. Special.

She set her soda on the counter. "I'm trying to say a place's beauty isn't about the trappings. It's about appreciating it exactly as it is."

"That's pretty profound, actually." Her sister stood beside her, leaning back against the counter, quietly waiting.

So much more effective than if her sister had pressed.

"The media paints Troy as this arrogant, urbane guy." She thought of that first time she'd seen him on the plane. "It's a face he puts on for the world, and honestly that persona is sexy as hell."

Her sister raised one eyebrow and waved for Hillary to keep talking.

"But the real person underneath it all is infinitely more fascinating." So much so, she didn't know how she would ever get over him.

"You're in love with him."

"Completely," she answered without hesitation.

"Then why isn't he here?"

Such a simple question.

He wasn't with her because…?

She'd pushed him away. Yes, he'd lied to her. He wasn't a perfect man. God knows, she wasn't perfect, either. Just because he'd screwed up, that didn't mean everything about their week together had been false.

Life wasn't all or nothing for either of them. They would need time together to build a relationship, to learn to trust each other. She understood that now.

But would Troy understand it, as well—if she got a second chance to tell him?

"You owe me for this, Colonel." Troy rocked back on his heels, jamming his fists in his tuxedo pockets to keep from punching a wall in frustration over having to hang out at a black-tie fundraiser.

Less than two weeks had passed since he and the colonel had come to Chicago, and already the man was calling again, asking him to show his face at this dinner dance for some reason he'd yet to disclose.

In D.C.

Which happened to be the last place on earth Troy wanted to be since it reminded him of Hillary. He just wanted to go back to Costa Rica and lock himself in his man cave for some serious alone time. Except he couldn't go back to Costa Rica, not when he'd made love to her in every corner of the place, his home so full of memories he'd been climbing the walls without her.

Salvatore clapped him on the back as the jazz band fired up a Broadway show tune. "Actually, I don't owe you a thing. The way I remember it, you owe me."

"Our agreement didn't include back-to-back gigs." Even if this one was a good cause, hosted by Senator Landis to raise money for the area Big Brother program for at-risk and foster kids. "In spite of my playboy rep, I do have to work."

"Just pretend for a couple of hours, then your time will be your own for at least…oh, let's say six months." Salvatore held up his hand. "I promise."

Troy angled to the side for a waiter carrying a silver tray of appetizers to pass before saying to the colonel, "With all due respect, you lie."

Salvatore adjusted his red tie. "I take offense at that. Lying is a very dishonorable trait."

Troy ground his teeth. Had the colonel been hired by Hillary to call attention to all his flaws?

Then as if conjured from his thoughts, he saw her across the room. *Hillary.* She wore a simple black dress with complete elegance, outshining every other woman in the room. His fist clenched the diamond pendant tighter—her necklace—that he'd been carrying around in his pocket since she left him on the island. What were the odds he would see her at the first place he went after leaving Costa Rica?

The odds were off the charts, in fact.

"Damn it, Colonel." He glared at Salvatore. "Did you set this up? You want me to crawl back to her? She made it clear she doesn't want me. She doesn't trust me. That's all there is to it."

"Bull."

His head snapped back. "What did you just say?"

"You heard me. You're a smart man. A genius, actually, part of why I work with you. But you're also manipulative. You use that brain to trick people into doing what you want, while making them think it was their idea. Another reason you're a great asset to my team. But that kind of game playing does not go over well in relationships."

"I have friends."

"Who play by your same convoluted—sometimes sketchy—rules." Salvatore gripped him on the shoulder in a move that was almost...fatherly? "Here with Hillary, you had a chance at a normal, healthy relationship, and you blew it. Any clue why?"

"You seem to have all the answers today. You tell me." And God, he actually meant it. He wanted help, to find a way to get her back because the past days without her had been pure hell.

"I can't give you all the answers. If you want her bad enough, you'll figure this one out on your own. Which you can do if you use that genius brain of yours and think." He tapped Troy's temple. "Why are you here when she's here?"

"Because you set us up."

Salvatore shook his head. "Think again."

With a final pat on Troy's shoulder, the colonel faded into the crowd.

Could Hillary have actually called the colonel and asked for his help? Why would she have reached out to Salvatore rather than him?

That answer was easy enough. He'd made himself inaccessible to everyone except Salvatore. He'd hidden away in his cave and used all his techie toys to make himself unreachable.

Hillary had told him from the start she had trust issues

and he'd pushed that one inexcusable button. It was almost like his subconscious had self-destructed the relationship. For a man of reason, that was tough to swallow.

But love wasn't about logic. Hell, his feelings for Hillary were definitely not anything rational. He just loved her, and he wanted her. And he intended to do everything in his power to win her back.

Click.

The cool metal wrapped around his wrist. He barely had time to register the sensation before he looked up and found Hillary standing beside him.

Click.

She locked the other handcuff around her wrist.

Hillary hoped the smile on Troy's face was for real and not an act for the crowd. A spotlight focused on them as she led him across the ballroom floor. The partiers applauded while the senator took the mic from the lead singer in the band to thank Troy Donavan for his very generous donation.

That part had been Salvatore's idea—when she'd contacted him begging for help in finding Troy. She'd been surprised to learn from Salvatore that he and Troy actually worked together on a more regular basis—but it made sense. She'd already realized there was more to the man she loved than the superficial. And even as a teen, he hadn't cared what the world thought of him. He'd been out there crusading in his own way. She was glad now that she hadn't known before about his work with Interpol. That would have made it too easy to trust him. She wouldn't have had to search her heart and open her eyes.

Salvatore had even made her a job offer she found more than a little tempting...leave her D.C. position and sign on to freelance with Interpol. She and Troy had a lot to talk about. Thank goodness Salvatore had worked out a plan for her to speak to him. Granted, something a little less high profile would have been easier on her nerves. But Salvatore had insisted this would work best.

Hillary searched for a private corner, but there were people everywhere. Finally, she tugged him down the corridor and into a powder room—and, as she'd hoped, the presence of a man chased both of the occupants out. She passed the bathroom attendant folded cash and said, "Could you give us ten minutes alone, please?"

Laughing under her breath, the attendant ducked out into the hall. Hillary locked the door after them and turned back to Troy only to find herself at a loss.

She'd been so focused on getting him alone and making her gesture meaningful. She'd even planned at least three speeches…all of which flew out of her head now that she was face-to-face with him. So she gave herself a moment to just soak in the beloved sight of him, here, with her again.

God, he knew how to wear a tuxedo, with the white silk scarf and fedora. He stole her breath as well as her thoughts.

Troy held up their wrists. "You sure do know how to make an impression."

"I wanted to make sure neither of us could run away this time."

"Good move." He stroked the inside of her wrist with his thumb. "How is your mother?"

The past couple of days had been hectic, getting her mom settled in with hospice home care, talking during her lucid moments. "She and I have done a lot of speaking again. We're finding a way to make peace." As much as was possible, but they were trying. "But that's not why I'm here tonight. Troy, I want to tell you—"

He pressed a finger to her lips.

"You know what? Hold that thought." He cupped her waist and lifted her onto the bathroom counter next to a basket of rolled-up hand towels. "I need to say some things to you first. Any objections?"

Smiling hopefully, she held up their cuffed wrists and jingled the cuffs. "You have my undivided attention."

"For starters, you left this." He pulled his free hand from his pocket. Her diamond cow necklace dangled from his fingertips. "It belongs to you."

A smile played with her lips and her heart. "I'm guessing there aren't a lot of women on the lookout for one of those."

"It's a one-of-a-kind, made for a one-of-a-kind woman." He reached behind her neck, taking her cuffed hand along as he latched her necklace in place again.

The charm still carried his heat as it rested against her chest.

He clasped their hands between them. "You've taught me a lot, Hillary Wright."

"What would that be?"

"I've prided myself on being fearless in business, fearless in standing up for a cause, even if it lands me in hot water." He linked hands with her. "But I botched things when it really counted. When it comes to relationships—when it came to the way I handled things with you—I haven't grown much beyond the kid who hid in his computer room rather than risk having people let him down. I betrayed your trust, and I'm so very sorry for that."

There hadn't been many people in his life teaching *him* how to trust when he was growing up. "The fact that I'm here should tell you something. I forgive you for not telling me right away, and I hope you'll forgive me for running rather than talking through things."

"Thank God." His throat moved in a long slow swallow.

His eyes slid closed, and she realized how, in spite of his grins and jokes, he really was sweating this every bit as much as she was. She mattered to him.

She rested her forehead against his.

Troy threaded his fingers through her hair. "You're a hundred percent right to demand I pony up my one hundred percent where you're concerned. You deserve it all, everything, and I want to be the man who makes that happen for you. I need to tell you something else, about Colonel Salvatore and—"

"Your freelance work with Interpol?"

"How did you…? He told you, didn't he?"

"Yes, he did, when I asked him to help me find you."

Troy eyed her warily. "And you're not upset with me for not explaining it myself? I know how important trust is to you."

"I'm assuming that kind of work isn't something you just go around sharing with people right away, but you'll have to clue me in on the nuances since it looks like I'll be signing on with the colonel, as well. He says his recruit list needs some estrogen."

For once, she'd stunned Troy into complete silence. His jaw went slack, and he started to talk at least twice, only to stop and shove his hand through his long hair. Finally, he just smiled and laughed. He wrapped his unshackled arm around her and spun her once before setting her on her feet again.

"God, I love you, Hillary. No questions or doubts in my mind, I am so in love with you." He kissed her once, twice then held on the third time until her knees went weak. "You know I'm going to want to be with you on any assignment so I don't go crazy worrying. Maybe I should be more laid-back, but when it comes to you—"

"You already are everything I could want, and of course we'll be together, always, so I can watch your back," she said against his mouth, her heart so full she could barely breathe. "I love you, too, Troy, my totally original man. Mine."

"Yes, ma'am, I am." He kissed her, firmly, intensely, holding for at least seven heartbeats. "I intend to work on being the best man possible for you each and every day." He sketched kisses over her forehead, along her eyes, finishing on the tip of her nose. "I'm a smart man, you know. I'll figure this one out if you'll give me the time."

"How much time were you thinking about?"

"A lifetime."

She took his hat and dropped it on her head. "It just so happens, that totally works for me."

* * * * *

REQUEST YOUR FREE BOOKS!
2 FREE NOVELS PLUS 2 FREE GIFTS!

Harlequin®

Desire

ALWAYS POWERFUL, PASSIONATE AND PROVOCATIVE

YES! Please send me 2 FREE Harlequin Desire® novels and my 2 FREE gifts (gifts are worth about $10). After receiving them, if I don't wish to receive any more books, I can return the shipping statement marked "cancel." If I don't cancel, I will receive 6 brand-new novels every month and be billed just $4.30 per book in the U.S. or $4.99 per book in Canada. That's a saving of at least 14% off the cover price! It's quite a bargain! Shipping and handling is just 50¢ per book in the U.S. and 75¢ per book in Canada.* I understand that accepting the 2 free books and gifts places me under no obligation to buy anything. I can always return a shipment and cancel at any time. Even if I never buy another book, the two free books and gifts are mine to keep forever.

225/326 HDN FEF3

Name	(PLEASE PRINT)	
Address		Apt. #
City	State/Prov.	Zip/Postal Code

Signature (if under 18, a parent or guardian must sign)

Mail to the **Reader Service:**

IN U.S.A.: P.O. Box 1867, Buffalo, NY 14240-1867
IN CANADA: P.O. Box 609, Fort Erie, Ontario L2A 5X3

Not valid for current subscribers to Harlequin Desire books.

Want to try two free books from another line?
Call 1-800-873-8635 or visit www.ReaderService.com.

* Terms and prices subject to change without notice. Prices do not include applicable taxes. Sales tax applicable in N.Y. Canadian residents will be charged applicable taxes. Offer not valid in Quebec. This offer is limited to one order per household. All orders subject to credit approval. Credit or debit balances in a customer's account(s) may be offset by any other outstanding balance owed by or to the customer. Please allow 4 to 6 weeks for delivery. Offer available while quantities last.

Your Privacy—The Reader Service is committed to protecting your privacy. Our Privacy Policy is available online at www.ReaderService.com or upon request from the Reader Service.

We make a portion of our mailing list available to reputable third parties that offer products we believe may interest you. If you prefer that we not exchange your name with third parties, or if you wish to clarify or modify your communication preferences, please visit us at www.ReaderService.com/consumerschoice or write to us at Reader Service Preference Service, P.O. Box 9062, Buffalo, NY 14269. Include your complete name and address.

HDES11B

Enjoy this sneak peek of USA TODAY *bestselling author*
Maureen Child's newest title
UP CLOSE AND PERSONAL

Available September 2012 from Harlequin® Desire!

"**L**aura, I know you're in there!"

Ronan Connolly pounded on the bright blue front door, then paused to listen. Not a sound from inside the house, though he knew too well that Laura was in there. Hell, he could practically *feel* her standing just on the other side of the damned door.

He glanced at her car parked alongside the house, then glared again at the still-closed front door.

"You won't convince me you're not at home. Your car is parked in the street, Laura."

Her voice came then, muffled but clear. "It's a driveway in America, Ronan. You're not in Ireland, remember?"

"More's the pity." He scrubbed one hand across his face and rolled his eyes in frustration. If they were in Ireland right now, he'd have half the village of Dunley on his side and he'd bloody well get her to open the door.

"I heard that," she said.

Grinding his teeth together, he counted to ten. Then did it a second time. "Whatever the hell you want to call it, Laura, your car is *here* and so are you. Why not open the door and we can talk this out. Together. In private."

"I've got nothing to say to you."

He laughed shortly. That would be a first indeed, he told himself. A more opinionated woman he had never met. He had to admit, he had enjoyed verbally sparring with her. He admired a quick mind and a sharp tongue. He'd admired her even more once he'd gotten her into his bed.

HDEXP0912

He glanced down at the dozen red roses he held clutched in his right hand and called himself a damned fool for thinking this woman would be swayed by pretty flowers and a smooth speech. Hell, she hadn't even *seen* the flowers yet. At this rate, she never would.

Huffing out an impatient breath, he lowered his voice. "You know why I'm here. Let's get it done and have it over then."

There was a moment's pause, as if she were thinking about what he'd said. Then she spoke up again. "You can't have him."

"What?"

"You heard me."

Ronan narrowed his gaze fiercely on the door as if he could see through the panel to the woman beyond. "Aye, I heard you. Though, I don't believe it. I've come for what's mine, Laura, and I'm not leaving until I have it."

Will Ronan get what he's come for?

Find out in Maureen Child's new title
UP CLOSE AND PERSONAL

Available September 2012 from Harlequin® Desire!

HARLEQUIN *Presents*

The scandal continues
in The Santina Crown miniseries
with *USA TODAY* bestselling author

Sarah Morgan

Second in line to the throne, Matteo Santina
knows a thing or two about keeping his cool under
pressure. But when pop star singer Izzy Jackson
shows-up to her sister's wedding and makes
a scandalous scene that goes against all royal
protocol, Matteo whisks her offstage, into his limo
and straight to his luxury palazzo.... Rumor has it
that they have yet to emerge!

DEFYING THE PRINCE

Available August 21 wherever books are sold!

HP13090

HARLEQUIN®

SYTYCW
SO YOU THINK YOU CAN WRITE

Harlequin and Mills & Boon are joining forces in a global search for new authors.

In September 2012 we're launching our biggest contest yet—with the prize of being published by the world's leader in romance fiction!

Look for more information on our website, **www.soyouthinkyoucanwrite.com**

So you think you can write? Show us!